MAN'S WARS & WICKEDNESS:
A Book of Proposed Remedies and Extreme Formulations for Curing Hostility, Rivalry, and Ill-Will

Amanda Ackerman &
Harold Abramowitz

//
[bon aire projects]

//

Man's Wars & Wickedness: A Book of Proposed Remedies & Extreme
Formulations for Curing Hostility, Rivalry, And Ill-Will
© 2017 Amanda Ackerman & Harold Abramowitz

ISBN: 978-0-9915820-2-0

//

ACKNOWLEDGEMENTS

The authors wish to thank the editors of Area Sneaks and Outward
From Nothingness where early excerpts from this work were previously
published.

The authors also wish to thank Amanda Montei and Jon Rutzmoser.
Michelle Detorie. Janice Lee. Andrea Quaid. Deb Perlman. Erica Lewis.
Theodore Abramowitz. Nathan Abramowitz. Sharone Abramowitz.

//

www.bonaireprojects.com

For the corn

MAN'S WARS & WICKEDNESS:

A Book of Proposed Remedies and Extreme

Formulations for Curing Hostility, Rivalry, and Ill-Will

THE DAUGHTER SOUGHT OUT TO STUDY STAYING POWER SCIENTIFICALLY.

It begins with the way things often begin, and that is with the way things are. Either something is in the process of staying or in the process of leaving, or evaporating. Even that which is not disposable. Like a good solid table. Even that which is supposed to be sturdy, like a good solid table, is in the process of leaving this earth. Either you want something to stay, and keep on staying, or to begin its process of dissent. Or its descent into decay. Because everything is perfect in itself, but either a poison or a benefit to another. Such as a cultural monument, like the great ones of all Europe. The daughter's name is Samantha and her mother is dead. Samantha is also the one and only true love of Lord Burlington, and she has decided that, as lovers, they are a benefit to each other and not poisonous. Samantha decides this is a good starting place. My mother, an immigrant, thinks Samantha, traveled to see the great cultural monuments of all of Europe when she was alive. And all the old and new buildings and all the tarry alleyways. She looped a camera around her neck with a nylon strap. The strap never broke. But does it have staying power, or is it in the process of decay? Samantha lives on Lord Burlington's estate. Right now, there is a Blue Ox sitting by the pool. She has lived here for four years and recently Samantha has gifted her with an amber necklace to bring out the burgundy in her eyes. Upon receiving the necklace, the Blue Ox said to Samantha, This gift is a mark of your character. You are now on your way to becoming generous and free. I hope you did not spend all your money though, the Blue Ox says without irony. Samantha thought that was a good place to begin. The Blue Ox eats grass, but my mother. My mother tried new foods. Gooseberry bread. And now she is dead. But do any of these thoughts help? thinks Samantha. I very much want them to. Samantha is writing a manifesto. There are many manifestos in the world these days, but Samantha is sitting outside, facing the world. The hills are green again, the fire in her heart is blue, and therefore Samantha is in the process of attempting to make a single true statement. And so she goes on thinking, imagining herself untying knots, the ones clouding her head. My mother, thinks Samantha, loved traveling in order to see cultural monuments. Because they have been granted staying power. And there is always someone there, a worker of sorts, someone who works with plaster or brick or blueprints, or someone who makes cider, or someone who shovels the cement, or someone who walks kindly down the halls, who will be there to fix the monuments if they begin to fall apart. These men, and they are usually men, have various powders and paints and building supplies they use in order to make the cultural monument better, plate glass, for example, and intellectual power, and the point is to make something better and not worse. The point is to prevent decay. Lord Burlington, however, thinks Samantha is not writing a manifesto but a case study of someone who's dead, her mother. He calls it *Case Study #31*, or rather, *In the Alleyways, in the Forests, and on the Head of the Ocean*, or rather, *Gratefully Putting Poisons in Your Sack*. Samantha is sitting outside next to the Blue Ox. Samantha is wearing a dress of tomato-colored velvet and looking at her reflection in Lord Burlington's pool. My mother, who was an immigrant, thinks Samantha…claimed that pigs ate human trash, claimed that peacocks ate lizards and not grasses, such as wild barleygrass, when they wanted to be nourished. She would have eaten anything, my mother. And now she is gone. Since she is dead, she now dwells in the Great Stomach, where she cooks and works. And still there she is, believing in staying power, believing in the staying power of the cultural monument. The great ones of all of Europe. Sometimes they are buildings and sometimes they are forests. My mother thinks the forests are cultural monuments. She takes pictures of them. She hangs the camera around her neck. These adventures in travel give her, she says, the ability to cancel out the poisons. She is grateful to the people who make the monuments last, who make them better.

YOU ATTEMPTED TO SCIENTIFICALLY STUDY WHAT.

Manifestos? Well, yes, I would say that you are sick, Mr. Jones. I would say that, if truth be told. Dr. Honorable is picking his teeth with a toothpick. If sickness and death are what you want, Jones, then I would say that you are sick. What you wanted? What you wanted. That is, manifestos found on the street. But I asked you about this before I died, says Mr. Jones. I asked you, Doctor, and you wouldn't tell me. We were walking down the street. Don't you remember? It was dark. There was no time. Time was wasting, I tell you. The way the fire burns. Gazebos are on fire. It is a vision of the future. But it still burns. And the burning is repellent. But it attracts. And burning is attractive. But it still burns. And I can't stand to hear you talk that way, Mr. Jones. It's defeatist. A defeatist attitude, I tell you. And, well, you've already lost the game, so what is the point of having a defeatist attitude now? It is a little bit, shall we say, self-indulgent, and especially so coming from someone already dead. What way? asks Mr. Jones. That way? So mystical. Building your city, your country, your whole society out of very attractive stones. I mean, come on. It was never that way. I looked down. I found a manifesto lying on the street. There was a street. A million pages, at least. There were millions and millions of pages lying on the street, waiting to be picked up. It wasn't brilliant at all. In fact, it wasn't anything. You could do with a rest, my friend, says Dr. Honorable. You could do with a cure. Yep, that's it, a cure. A cure. Rest. Bedrest. That's exactly what you need. Or, shall we say, exactly what you *did* need. That is, if it wasn't already too late. If you weren't already deceased, or, rather, dead! What I need! And what would you know about what I need, Honorable? What? I ask you, exclaims Mr. Jones. And there is something extraordinary on the street. They can see it, that is, people can see it, if they look carefully. A tree, perhaps. Perhaps, it is a tree. And they could find its value in virtue. The stuff that virtue is made of. But you say you saw this on the street? You say you picked up a page and began reading? You say this because you want a job? Because you want a cure? Because you want to find the way to the thermal spring waters, to the good Dalmatian or Salmatian salts, the green kind, and to the healthiest region in all Europe?

THE ESOTERIC SOUGHT OUT TO STUDY THE HEALTHIEST REGION IN ALL EUROPE SCIENTIFICALLY.

Tonight the world feels a bit tossed. *But everyone around me looks so attractive*, thinks the esoteric. The air ripples. It is evening and the esoteric is dining alone. It is not observant of everything—like the curtains or the silverware or the coats hanging on a hat-stand by the doorway—but it is excellent at noticing people's moods or beliefs and what is generally important about them. The esoteric has volcanic ash for eyes, a harp for a brain, cloaked teeth, and a grape-colored belt. *But my heart is open, more than most. My heart is on a string. And that in itself is a political act. Won't you see?* It observes: *This is a good night to realize that you are in no way obliged to suffer. I came from the body and work of man and like any microcosm I can become grainy and green, or dry out at a moment's notice if you forget me. Except that I, being esoteric, have to move with the seasons, the cosmological revolutions and cosmological order, and thus consume in the fall, grow thin in the winter, then eat in the summer and grow fat again. It is a nice life; it has exactly the right amount of struggle attached to it. And I will tell you where to go so that you can erase your misery. The Swabian coast. The healthiest region in all Europe. It has dry sand and saunas, good salts, hearty ferns, clean skies, and aloe vera plants. It was discovered countless years ago by a young Swabian girl who wore her hair in a chaotic braid. She had found the coast accidentally, or so she said, but no sooner had she made the discovery then all the sunbathers and day-trippers, people with parasols and baseball caps, began to come in swarms, each with their own size and thickness, all looking to be cured, because they were all so miserable and sick, and they all brought wallets, and some wallets were thick and some*

were thin. The little girl had told them, because they were rampant consum-
ers, 'You should know this: if another summer does not come, all men (and
women too), like microcosms, will dry out. None of you should be so bold and
foolish.' But, the esoteric continues to think, *I couldn't resist the Swabian*
coast. I wrapped myself in a cloak of black figs, tried to look shade-bound,
and set up a booth on the shore. I called myself a doctor. I had my righteous
designs. After all I had been designed within the black stars and blue mists
and orchid groves. I tasted the waters and mineral springs, measured their
dilutions of salt, waded through the plants, got my slender white gloves dirty
and wet. And the people were impressed. They paid good money for my ad-
vice, which is, of course, a totally political act. That's why some love Esoteric
cures, while others hate them—take Dr. Honorable for example, he thinks
I'm charging too much for my heathen cures. He wants to put me in jail, or at
least to see me publicly shamed, character assassinated, lashed with goose-
berry branches, called a girl, a squirt, a skirt, a sissy. But I have pursued a
doctorate degree of my own making: I am now an expert on the four external
limbs, the microcosm, food and drink, and all that will befall man. If only
someone will—No, Jones, no, just no! cries Doctor Honorable. You are trying to push me away, hit me where it hurts so I don't cure you! And you say
you found this manifesto in the street? You are challenging my most sacred
beliefs. And still, I shall never desert you.

THE STRANGER ATTEMPTED TO STUDY THE WALK SCIENTIFICALLY.

And it is strange when they walk that way. And they are walking a lot at night these days. It is strange to be stuck in such a place at such a time, thinks Mr. Jones. It is strange. Or was strange. Or is strange still, but then, I'm confused. There are manifestos on the street. There are salespeople trying to sell plants and seeds, amazing plants and seeds, they claim, millions and millions of them, and, as usual, the salespeople are speaking and speaking and not listening to what they are saying, not paying attention to how their words, i.e., their salespitches, jingles, advertising, are going over with their own potential customers or the world at-large. And this becomes a flood. You could have had a different outcome, you know, Jones, says Dr. Honorable. There were any number of possibilities available at the time. It is not often that Dr. Honorable will extend his considerable services to one who is not in direct need of them, that is, to one who is already dead. But, in the special case of Mr. Jones, Dr. Honorable is happy to make an exception. And besides, it has been a slow morning, and he has nothing better to do. You didn't have to look down, Jones. You could have simply trusted your fate. I mean something would have happened eventually. You didn't have to know the specific course. And now it has transformed anyway. It has transformed without you. In fact, truth be told, it is spoken about in glowing terms these days, if you know what I mean. Know what I mean? Do you know what I mean, Mr. Jones? And how is it that you even know about me? asks Mr. Jones. Hey, do you want to know about the cure or not, Jones? I don't have all day. How you can even find the energy to pretend, at this point, is beyond me. You are a case study, Mr. Jones. An anomaly.

Dr. Honorable sighs. There is a beautiful view of the rolling hills of Swabia on the horizon. There is a beautiful view of the sea. Medicine and fixes and cures and the problems of medicine and fixes and cures disappear within the beautiful view. Still, one can't see things clearly. One can't see things clearly because there are millions and millions of pages blowing around everywhere. Manifestos, prescriptions for cures, lost knowledge, various medical tracts, the remnants, the cast-offs, the residue and reminders of the stupid fucking war filling up every space. It has become a flood. A disaster of epic proportions. I am scared, says Mr. Jones. What are you scared of? asks Dr. Honorable. I am scared of sickness and disease and malaise and stagnation and depression. Really? Dr. Honorable is surprised. You never seem scared. You really are scared, Jones? Really? I am scared, or I am tired. I tried to talk to you about it before. Actually, at our last appointment, if you remember. I did try. I saw those books, the manifestos, the medical tracts, and that unfinished translation of the Bible, with my own two eyes. In fact, the street was full of millions and millions of books. They looked flimsy. I remember thinking that it was lucky the wind wasn't blowing. Thus, what we have here is a case, thinks Dr. Honorable, shaking his head as if to ward off evil. And I shall call this case, *Case Study #193*, or rather, *It Is Very Powerful to Attempt to Fix That Which Is Broken.*

BECAUSE WE SHARE THE SAME ATMOSPHERE, THE SWABIAN PAPER MILL SOUGHT OUT TO STUDY AND ASSOCIATE ITS PRODUCTS WITH ECOLOGICALLY SOUND PRACTICES SCIENTIFICALLY.

This could have been a manifesto fluttering in the street... There was trouble at the Swabian Paper Mill until... Turkeys that live free in the forests... We have chosen to associate some of our products with turkeys that are too fat to be fliers. Because they share the same atmosphere with free-flying turkeys, we have decided to associate our too-fat-to-fly turkeys with such free-flying turkeys in order to help our environment. Because some good people have chosen to help save the environment, we have chosen to associate with them. Since we share an atmosphere and hence are related to them in this way, we at the Swabian Paper Company have chosen such associations for our products in order to be helpful and caring. Additionally, because there are forces of peace in the world, we at the Swabian Rifle Company have chosen to manufacture the Peace Rifle to show our solidarity with this atmosphere that promotes peace and love.

THE MEDICAL TRACT sought out to study ENDLESS PAPERWORK scientifically.

Dr. Honorable has returned to work at the Swabian Medical College. He is lecturing, giving a demonstration of sorts in a large operating theater/ classroom. There are very few open seats. The Swabian medical students are generally excellent. Engaged. Well-meaning. A happy band, so to speak, happy for the privilege to learn what they are learning from someone as, seemingly, capable as Dr. Honorable. What we have here is a case, begins Dr. Honorable. A case study, if you will. In fact, I call this particular case study...ta da...*Case Study #193*, or rather, *It is Very Powerful to Attempt to Fix That Which Is Broken*... It doesn't work so well, does it, Jones? I mean, when you try to talk about it. And, by the way, don't think I didn't notice the way you looked at those pages. In fact, I don't blame you. Millions and millions of pages fluttering around in the street are a little hard not to envy. However, someone did have to write all that stuff, you know. And here you are just lying dead in your patch of grass, feeling hurt. Feeling neglected. Don't you get that other people feel the same things you feel, Mr. Jones? Why, it's universal! Why, everything is connected! Just think of the poor fool who lost all those pages in the first place. Manifestos, prescriptions for cures, arcane knowledge, various medical tracts, for crying out loud. A manifesto! A magnum opus, by the looks of it. And, what's more, you don't even seem to realize the pressure I'm under. The way I've extended myself on your behalf. The service to humankind I'm performing by treating you! Jones, you can't even begin to imagine the effort it takes to treat, or rather, nurture that which is already dead and gone. By Jove, it is easy to forget, yet one must never forget! And do you really think you are going to find anyone in the medical industry who cares besides me, Jones? And where would comparable high-quality treatment and care be found, pray tell? Growing on trees? Blowing around on the street? And for free, no less! Why, there isn't an insurance company in the land that would be willing to pay good money against such an obvious, and rather egregious, if you don't mind my saying, pre-existing condition? Death! Paper cuts! Manifestos! What the Hell is the difference! Indeed, any insurance company worth its name would be well within its rights if it chose to waste your eternity with endless paperwork just for thinking of making a claim against this. And what do you think the world would look like after that kind of delay, Mr. Jones? Manifestos? Lost knowledge? Various medical tracts? Lost prescriptions for cures? Millions and millions of pages? Why, that would be just the beginning!

THE SECRET REMEDY SOUGHT OUT TO STUDY CHARITABLE MOTIVES SCIENTIFICALLY.

The secret remedy had been living for eons under a small cherry tree. The two creatures lived in a tucked-away spot at the back of Lord Burlington's estate where no one ever walked. A grassy meadow. Occasionally the Blue Ox loped nearby but she didn't disrupt the order of things. Neither the tree nor the secret remedy did a whole lot during the day, but there were many gestures of care between them. Then the order of things changed and the cherry tree wept when the secret remedy boasted of its plans to see the world, its voice sounding partly like a grand piano and partly like a doctor and partly like an epithet for whatever you wanted it to mean. Secret remedy's desire proceeded from many firm assumptions about the world. For example, its first assumption was that there was a world. And was this world cause for shame or cause for hope? Did it have many diving birds and cliffs and trees and seaside activities? Cures? Places to dip your feet? The secret remedy was ready to turn its collar up and face the bracing winds. The cherry tree wept because it felt itself neglected (a mark of character it wanted to change but hadn't managed to yet). And so, upon the cherry tree's simple, authentic expression of emotion, The secret remedy took out its notebook and practiced making some observations: does the cherry tree have my best interests at heart? Is it a *charitable* creature? The cherry tree, suddenly finding itself an object of study and inquiry, wilted even more, like a piece of overgrown fruit dragging down its branch, like an overgrown horsetomato causing its own stem to sag—and we all know a stem is a home, or a cellulose chord, or lifeline, or lifetime. The secret remedy decided to leave the estate. As it tottered down the dusty road it could hear the cherry tree crooning and sighing in the background... *You know I don't believe you when you say that you don't need me...* The Secret Remedy wrote in its notebook: is song itself *charitable*? Does it give or does it only have the appearance of giving? Like all secret remedies, this secret remedy, when appropriately ingested or applied, could make the body better and not worse. It had a beneficial effect on nations even, for any country has a heart, liver, spleen, synovial fluid, or joints. Lord Burlington loved his crops of secret remedies, and even more, loved not sharing them. That is, with anyone but Samantha, his one and true love. The secret remedy decided it would be no man's property. But then it began to ache with fear. It wrote in its notebook: is the heart, well, truly *charitable*? Especially if no rain comes? Or what if the rain comes, but the sun dries itself out, and there is nothing to remove the moisture? What if the sun disappears entirely, and altogether? And then the waters, the heat, the ground, the air... all of it thrown off, entirely. And then the heart will be gone and the world will have to be remade. For the heart is dependent on... all is dependent on it. And what is there to measure without *charity*? When the secret remedy glanced back at the cherry tree, scraping its buds on ground, it thought, *Have I killed the heart already?* My knowledge would be useless before I even began.

THE ROSE AT THE BACK OF THE HOUSE SOUGHT OUT TO STUDY ITS OWN BENEFICIAL EFFECT SCIENTIFICALLY.

And it was always that way. It was always going to be that way. You could have asked a clam and the clam would have told you a story. A real story. There is a beneficial effect in place here. Or you can't live long, not the way you've not been living, Mr. Jones. Or how it could have been, thinks Mr. Jones. There could have been trouble for the rose at the back of the house. The rose at the back of the house was generally very good, healthy, but was often projected upon wildly, and in a variety of ways. In fact, the rose at the back of the house was so often accused of being so many things, its true nature remained a mystery, even, alas, unto itself. But vigilant you are not, Jones, says Dr. Honorable. And you are not ready to go home either. You are not ready to buy a house. And you are accused of committing terrible crimes. And you are, at least, at the very least, guilty of at least two very serious crimes, albeit misdemeanors. I can't believe it, Jones. I can't believe that I am forced to have to explain things to you, over and over again. After all, you are dead, and I am a physician! But you forgot the rose at the back of the house. Its true nature. Its beneficial effect. Science. The potential for dropsy. The potential cure. Not that you feel any of those symptoms now, do you, Jones? Dr. Honorable asks a lot of his patients. He expects to have a pretty clear picture of the state of their health in advance of the various treatments he provides. In fact, Dr. Honorable's clinic was once near a prison, and he has brought poison, beneficial poison, automatically, having forgotten that his patient, Mr. Jones, is already dead. Still, it is very beneficial to medicine, to the whole concept of medicine, when the dead and gone, so to speak, come home to roost. And you couldn't hear me, Jones, could you? Asks Dr. Honorable. I was talking to you. I was at a very critical point in your treatment when you stopped being a good patient, if you recall. And, the next thing you knew, you were dead. And now I'm dead, sighs Mr. Jones. I don't know how everything got so very mixed up. Dr. Honorable smiles, nods his head, and, just in case, secretly sprinkles the beneficial poison he has brought in the air as Mr. Jones reminisces. There was a new position. A feeling that the times were very good, very auspicious for certain things. Still, there was the distinct feeling that I had to leave. And that was on a Tuesday. The very day before I was diagnosed with dropsy. Incredible pain. Ahem! But the rose at the back of the house. The garden. The beneficial effect. Perfect attendance. A happy band of medical students. And for naught. All for naught! The remainder of the day all used up, booked up, so to speak. And there is a message waiting unread. And you have an unexpected visitor. But the beneficial effect. The romance of the rose at the back of the house. A secret remedy hidden away in the garden. A potential cure. And well in advance of any symptoms! And ladies and gentlemen, this rose at the back of the house. The very one you see here, has, indeed, been, or, rather, is possessed by, a beneficial effect. Beneficial, I tell you. It was in her eyes, Doctor, every time she looked at me. But, right now, I could sure use a cup of water. Pray, Doctor, that the entire medical industry, the pharmaceutical giants, especially, don't come and take me away too soon. I might still be of some use to science, to research, at least. In any case, I wanted to thank you all for being here, continues Jones. You are all very good students, no doubt. And to prove it, we will, at some point in the very near future, observe this beautiful glass cover being put back over the rose at the back of the house. We will, heaven's permitting, watch it being lowered over the rose together. Did I thank you all for coming? Did I tell you that the rose at the back of the house was beneficial? Let me apologize for repeating myself, but I think I may need another glass of water.

THE PROCESS OF DIGESTION DECIDED TO STUDY COUNTERCULTURE SCIENTIFICALLY.

It knew what counterculture was not: a car, a carport, a folding chair, a piece of candy, a crisis, a patient, a physician, pain, the pharmaceutical industry, an act of violence, bodily harm, or an acting mayor. But it did not yet know what counterculture was: was it the rose at the back of the house rising up inside its glass jar, a good recovery, a modest fee, a damaging lampoon, a mountaintop, a new approach to nature, vegetable mush? The Acting Mayor of All Swabia, Tom Terrific, was not offended by these observations. He wanted to be associated with culture only. It was good to be associated with culture. Helpful for his career. Counterculture was definitely not a gooseberry-colored tie. A wide grin. But he did add, if one can associate oneself with culture, and not counterculture, then one can hope for and expect a good recovery—if one finds this world intolerable they are always going to be sick. I did not believe him. Instead, I subscribed wholly to the advice of the processes of my digestion, for I always knew when my stomach was oppressed. There is a cavity and a sense of wobbliness, prickliness, or burning. Red, more red, and yes, more red. And you don't want that growing in your stomach, believe me. You will starve, you will have to live on the bottom of a cave and dwell there and starve. This—acting so, *primitive*, so to speak—this foraging for gooseberries, or scrounging for weeds, for trash, for whatever you can find, is not a return to nature or a new approach to nature. And for everything I eat, something as good or better must replace it the next time I eat, if I am to stay well and not become unhealthy. And should I become sick, I mean really sick, really uncomfortable, even to the point where I can't function, can barely walk or stand up or think, I want a good recovery. The right medicine. The right cure. What if I get dropsy? Or worse? And I cannot compel culture to do this, to do this for me, to make me better, to make me well, for it is—and sometimes is not—subject to the desires and appetites of humanity. Therefore, today, in the case of human disease and discontentment, one must practice the art of counterculture. Of making it exist. That way you're having the right reaction to an intolerable world. And so it was that the processes of digestion urged me to find a brisk mountaintop, a rose at the back of the house, thermal spring waters, good Dalmatian or Salmatian salts, the green kind, and the healthiest region in all Europe. The best thing for your digestion is a long walk. Try to take at least two a day. And tend carefully to the lymphatic tissue. It's as delicate as a fringed yellow orchid, and fussy too. And so I was compelled to quit my car, cast away my folding chair, and stand on my own two feet. I am on to the next page of my a million-and-such-pages long manifesto. Here is my damaging lampoon of the now acting mayor…

A NEW APPROACH TO NATURE SOUGHT OUT TO STUDY THERAPEUTIC BATHING AND MEDICINAL SPRINGS SCIENTIFICALLY.

A secret remedy, or why things heal, or the way things just keep getting better and better all the time. It was in the autumn, and there was a grassy meadow. It was in the autumn and there were millions and millions of Swabian citizens involved in a variety of great commercial undertakings. For example, Tom Terrific, the Acting Mayor of All of Swabia, is very interested in the water. The way the water flows. Its ways and means. The thermal spring waters come to Swabia from the healthiest region in all Europe. Yet, the healthiest region in all Europe is very far away? Did I ever tell you the story of the water, Esmeralda, says Tom. How I had to hike all day? The going was hard, but there were therapeutic springs at the top of the mountain. In a cave, no less! I soon found that I couldn't go on. Yet I had to go on. Still, I couldn't go on and expect to stay in one place all the time. The mountains were a deep red. I tapped the walls of the cave with my walking stick. I sat in the water for days on end. I moved my feet. I touched my toes. I took therapeutic bath after therapeutic bath, and slept wonderfully. Sure, I would wake up all wet, but I'd had the presence of mind to bring along a towel. I was not afraid of success in the least. In fact, I believed that a miracle had come. The story gets better, says Tom Terrific, winking automatically at Esmeralda, his beloved. My whole quest for the water was based on principles newly discovered at that time. New approaches to nature. Secret remedies made known for the very first time. I was so enthusiastic. A veritable fool, my dear! I made myself go on. I had to go on. I made up chants, affirmations, rhymes, songs, limericks. Anything I wanted! Anything that would work. *My bladder is China.* Was how one went. *My spleen is Spain.* Was how another one went. And then I realized, I am entirely made up of landmasses—I am in the water for the very first time when I learn this. Tom Terrific leans out the window. The autumn wind blows cold. His story has left him somewhat breathless. A landmass, Esmeralda. Truly, a new approach to nature. And the natural waterfalls. And the thermal springs. And you, land. You, land, says Tom. Why, it is as if…as if… And you are really land when you come to that place and the water runs and the heat rises all over your body and you realize that you have finally found the most excellent way of maintaining one's health. I began composing a manifesto that day, Esmeralda. I stood at the top of the mountain and proclaimed to the sky, to the sun, to the very air: *I, Tom Terrific, am a citizen of the world and my body is made up of landmasses. I am made of ointment, of cures, and it is as if…as if…* Still, Esmeralda, it is very confusing when the sun, so to speak, sets on these kinds of moments in one's life. Why, the perfect moments just don't last. And the funny part is that even though you know the end is coming, it is still kind of sad and melancholy—a most melancholy moment—when it arrives. However, one has to be a good sport, or rather, one has to be realistic about these things. Take the good with the bad! And, really, it's perfectly understandable. New approaches to things *do* make a person just a little nervous. It's human nature! After all, we don't *really* have a way of knowing for sure, do we? The other shoe is bound to drop sometime! And that's why we have to stick together, Esmeralda, no matter what. The world asks so much of a person as it is. And what better reason to stay healthy, to boot! Be my beloved, Esmeralda…

I SOUGHT OUT TO STUDY MR. JONES SCIENTIFICALLY.

People said there was nobody like him. People said this over drinks at a bar, where those of us who were women were wearing long necklaces, and we said this even though the bar smelled uneven and inspiring, because all of those among us were like each other (in color, type, form, and fashion). Mr. Jones had a good manicure, raised the red asparagus on his fork, said good fortune comes from ability, the exercising of one's talent. He hated the summer. I never saw anyone hate the summer as much as Mr. Jones. I wanted to figure this out scientifically. I placed him one night in my mind's eye on a glass bed under a constellation, made him take off his left shoe but tie his right one in a perfect, thin, shoe-lace bow. I made him eat horsetomatoes. I made him cough and made him tell it like it is from the heart and made him pretend he played an obscure historical instrument that stood as a metaphor for heavenly bodies. I made him say that he was different, different from the rest of us, from the very universe, that no one had ever been or would ever be like him, a man rich in good gifts, with no fault of the blood, vividly real, glossy-skinned, right-acting, pinstriped, occasionally uptight, never irritating, glossy-lipped, an offering to the very firmament from which he was made. Lying on his back, on the glass table, which I had now turned to water, swimming and beginning to freeze, he said, Who knows what there is in the firmament that can serve us? The world began the way it began and everybody knows this. The world asks so much of a person and everybody knows this. He had the clarity of the sun. There was no one like him. He said, if you really want, I will pretend to be happy or unhappy while you undergo this very experiment, but remember, it is the fruit growing that makes the summer occur, and not the other way around. You control nothing in me, he said, but I will pretend, and I will pretend that I am the last man, the only man, that there is no one like me. He bowed, I think, but generously and effortlessly, and not anachronistically, and gave me a swig out of his beaker and a piece of his hair, allowed me to set it on fire, to watch it sway like seaweed in the water, to put it on a leash, to take it into the ocean, to wear it like a pin, to sleep with it under my pillow, to smell, and to look at it microscopically. To this day I have concluded that he is a fully constituted human being, a landmass. To this day I have found no one that replicates Mr. Jones in color, type, form, or fashion. He is unique. There is no one like him. He hates the summer and has the clarity of the sun.

POISON SOUGHT OUT TO STUDY THE FIVE WAYS OF GETTING SICK, DISEASE, SCIENTIFICALLY.

You have to realize that principles are at stake here, man... oh, sorry, I mean, mister... principles, I tell you, said Cecil one day to Mr. Jones. And the earth will not survive another cleansing, if you know what I mean, man. But Mr. Jones sneers because, at that moment, Mr. Jones is just the type of person to sneer. He is cleaning again, cleansing, if you will. And it hurts. This hurts. His story hurts. You've got to be careful when you are cleansing your heart, washing your hair, whatever, man. It's insane! And Mr. Jones was, indeed, a man, or rather, a fully constituted human being at one time, that's for sure. In fact, one could see the humanity in his walk, his gait, in the way he inhaled when he smoked a fig cigarette. His whole manner of being, for that matter. And, at one time, he'd had a special blue box, the good kind of blue, for his fig cigarettes and gold shoes and a fine walking stick. In fact, Mr. Jones was, at one time, very very handsome. I feel like crying right now, man, admits Cecil. I was always either in the process of staying, or of leaving, says Mr. Jones. And there were two or three things you had to know about my situation. You had to know how the cows felt about being on a grassy meadow all alone. How they felt about being left out there all alone. And on a grassy meadow, no less! And you had to know how it felt to be all alone at other times, too. Your soliloquy is wearing a little thin, man...oops, sorry, I mean, mister. You literally have nothing to live for and you haven't abandoned the melancholy yet? Oy, give it up already! Put on a happy face for once, for crying out loud! I get the appeal of melancholy, man, but even that gets a bit tiresome after a while. It's too much! exclaims Cecil. Why, it's as if...as if... You want a cure? Poison?

Disease? The five great stomach ailments? Cucumbers? Horsetomatoes? Well, I'll tell you this, first, you have to know how to marinate, mister. It's all about the sauce from day one, man. All about the sauce!

THE ARTICULATION OF SUFFERING SOUGHT OUT TO STUDY THE MAN WHO TURNED INTO A STORE SCIENTIFICALLY.

The man had previously been a highway, and many other things as well: stew, grass, stone, a deadly kind of blue, an inspiring song on the radio, even something as abstract as a closet. He liked himself. He liked being a store. He liked having people wander through and around him, the way desire made people roam. There was the noise to fill his hollow spaces. He didn't want to be friends with the articulation of suffering, who had won many friends through its articulations, but had also made many enemies. *I have given up on life but not melancholy.* It just rubbed some people the wrong way. This was to be expected—speak the truth and make someone your enemy. But on the other hand, hearing their suffering so perfectly articulated gave others the sense that they could understand their own times or circumstances, and this feeling sometimes even helped them to overcome their woes. Once they realized that their suffering was quite well defined, quite shared, there was gold, *The golden age of compassion will be me,* and they were healed permanently; thus, articulation of suffering was a controversial and oft-debated figure. Despite being so helpful (or unhelpful, depending on your point of view) the articulation of suffering couldn't, however, stomach a fish pond, it was too much even for the articulation of suffering to articulate: the moss, the crowdedness, the drudgery, the every day gurgling of the same water, and the same water with the same hosts of pletchy effluvium and barely moving tides, the baggage of stagnant algae, stone walls, bleak as bleak, mortared, swayed, lain, sometimes even in a backyard… The articulation of suffering couldn't bear to continue. It had given up on life but not on melancholy, so it pulled its striped red tie down over its sticky tongue, sucked on a sour candy, which turned all shades of sour (apple then grape then Milanese vanilla and lemon-lye, aniseed-and-grease, Carpathian bee-tongue, old Caribbean sand) then alternated the rest of the day just sitting in a chair, eating sweet stuff and then sour, sweet and then sour, sweet and then sour, until dusk. It looked out the window. It thought, The man who became a store is no longer afflicted. If the man who became a store could become the man who also turned into a fish pond, then I could have another truly miserable friend. He could help me define my suffering for me. After all, he has the stomach for it. I suppose I will need to manipulate him with my suffering. But really this was a misread of the situation. After all, the man who had turned into a store was drawn to nothing but suffering. Why else would he turn into a store, exporting and importing, being both host and guest, profiteer and spender, all the while maintaining an appealing outward appearance, and trying to sell and be sold to? In the end, all articulation of suffering needed to do was simply buy things from the man who turned into a store, it was so simple! But articulation of suffering, of course, was bad with cash, hopeless, sand through its fingers, hole in the pockets, and it couldn't see that the way forward was so simple, so at his disposal. It just involved money, the right price. If only the articulation of suffering could just see what was right in front of it.

THE FORM OF FASHION SOUGHT OUT TO STUDY THE MANY WAYS OF KNOWING SCIENTIFICALLY.

It started. Hollow. Flat-footed. Wearing a slip. And lovely hair, grown shaggy. And even then there was something wrong with Samantha, or so she thought. The world began in the way it began, but that was a long time ago, and everyone knows this, and no one questions this at all, at least not any more. But I found favor in this philosophy, thinks Samantha. And through it, I found favor in His eyes. In His religion, too, if truth be told. Yet there was something about the way He looked. The look in His eyes. And you were either in the process of staying, or of leaving. And I could have sworn he'd purchased that multi-colored gooseberry coat from the very same store in the village I'd seen it in that morning. You are false, man…I mean, mister…says Cecil with a grin. In fact, you never were anything but. Mr. Jones sighs and begins reciting his soliloquy: *There is a voice in your head that tells you what to do. You find favor. And the fact of favor is never amiss, never misses its mark when it really wants to tell you something. And I remember the way you used to dance close to the fire. I remember the way you used to hold your head up, but the mind drifts when it indulges itself in such thoughts. You were wearing a vest. I remember that. I remember the way you knew absolutely everything. You lived in an apartment and you always complained about the way the neighbors played their music too loudly. You wore a multi-colored blouse that had torn sleeves, and I was always so excited to see you. The music, the food, the dancing. The manifestos. The millions and millions of pages that had materialized out of thin air, that everyone seemed to be reading at the time. The multi-colored gooseberry coats that everyone was wearing that season…* And then Cecil begins to cry. And then

Samantha feels troubled. And there is torn fabric, millions and millions of multi-colored bits of it, floating everywhere. And there are seashells on the floor at the back of the poolhouse. Just outside the poolhouse, a gazebo is on fire. *I can't figure out how to get back to my room, continues Mr. Jones, and I am in the hall and I have been here before because I live here and now I am so sad I can't continue and I am convinced that I will start crying, too...* The clothes you wore were beautiful, thinks Samantha. But he doesn't deserve that compliment, sniffs Cecil, I do...*And self-doubt will destroy you, so to speak. Still, it was good to be wearing my multi-colored gooseberry coat again. But my eyes. My eyes refused to see what I was looking at, still, man, that jacket was loud. It had everyone on edge. I could see it in their eyes...*

THE DYNAMIC NOTION SOUGHT OUT TO STUDY THE FISH POND SCIENTIFICALLY.

The fish pond was round, about six feet in diameter, paved with blue tiles, and healthy; therefore, it was full of fish. The fish were of many sizes, colors, shapes and dispositions. Some were rancid with fear and others consummate keepers of the peace. The yellow ones especially. And in the fish pond there were also blue ones, and bottom feeders, shimmering ones, and ones with fins shaped like castles, who tended to be a bit on their high horse, arrogant, pretending that they were in a moat and not a fish pond. Dynamic notion wanted to stir things up a bit, everything had gotten too soft, too predictable, too stable, too staid. Dynamic notion liked dynamism, things moving forward, when you couldn't even catch your breath because life was like a big race, a cornucopia of sensations, chaos without crisis, places to see and riches to attract and wares to feel, and your head spins, and when you are spun you are reborn...Dynamic notion made an appeal to the heavens and to the stars, for the heavens of course are dynamic, and the stars always propelled in motion; they have poison in them. And everything exists at once in the world: bitter, sweet, sharp, wiry, acid, alkaline, fragile. And note how the stars can help the world, or contaminate it as well, and note that these contaminations are called poison, and note as well that there is no disease without a poison, and note that any disease causes change, often rapid change, whether healing or degenerate. After all, everything is either in the process of staying, or leaving. Or at least it should be, so one would think if one were a dynamic notion. And dynamic notion knew, because of its dynamism, that one mere substance could give rise to so many. If the sun got too hot the fish would die. If the world grew too cold the fish would die. How to strike just the right balance, how to strike the just-right forward push that would create momentum without outright and total devastation? He added a droplet of arsenic to the pond, just the right amount. And it gave rise to moss and algae and other entities: chocolate wrappers, special red bacteria, and so forth. The sun shone down. The fish with the flapping-castle fins mostly died, turned weaker, but something in their place was starting to come into being. A shift in the environment, a shift in the organisms that inhabit it, a new dream for the world.

THE DEPENDABLE END SOUGHT TO STUDY POISON SCIENTIFICALLY.

I put on a trusted suit, and then I ate out of the palm of your hand. Silence, Cecil! I am listening to a story, says Lord Burlington peevishly. And, by the way, your future ability to make a living depends on the truth of what I hear you say after the story is finished. So listen! A badger. Built-in plumbing. A wall-hanging. Dependable ends. Multi-colored garments. Ahem! Cecil, I strongly recommend that you put out that damned fig cigarette right now, dispense with your inane daydreaming, and listen! Think about your future, my boy. They sit back and listen to the story. *Once upon a time, the dependable end came to school sporting a brand new, very fancy, and very fashionable bag, and then promptly asked to be excused from the class it had just paid millions and millions in perfectly good Swabian currency to attend. Granted, the class had not been given in millions and millions of years, and thus the lesson would only have been understood in contemporary terms. But still, the dependable end was a jerk about such things and even worse about other things and never wished to be even tangentially associated with anyone else's ideas. The dependable end could be a real pill, and, because of this, there was often no tomorrow and no one ever remembered that they, too, were once called tomboys or imps or soda jerks or Tom Terrifics or every other name under the sun at one time or another. Still, any first-grader knows that ink, much less millions and millions of pages covered with ink, do not just materialize out of thin air. It's odd that we know each other at all, said dependable end's mysterious friend poison one day when they were sitting together on some large stones set in a grassy meadow. And, indeed, poison is something of a mystery: a weird and anomalous friend,*

poison was always mocking, was always losing its way, and, most of the time,
was very demanding. Dependable end, for its part, was, in addition to being
a jerk, or worse, sometimes overly self-absorbed and, truth be told, not the
best friend in the world: dependable end rarely had anything nice to say to
others, but loved to receive as much praise as possible. However, after long
periods, millions and millions of years, of being weird and even sometimes
competitive with one another, the tension would get to be too much and too
serious, and things would swing back the other way. Once upon a time, it
was a sunny day, and there were fantastic fortunes to be made in Swabia
and elsewhere. The dependable end and poison decided that they would stick
together no matter what, collaborate on projects forevermore, and attempt
to make a killing by patenting at least one of the things that was missing
from the world, but still generally thought to be desirable, e.g., the solution
to disgrace, the cure for disparagement, a scientific end to the problem of
loneliness, of not having an ample and always ready supply of clean clothes,
of not having a decent wardrobe at one's disposal... Well, Lord Burlington
yawns, if that's where all of this is going, I'm outta here! Cecil, forget about
those questions I was going to ask you. Get my car. I am going to take a
ride to the village. I am thinking of buying a new coat. What the kids call
a gooseberry coat, I think. Essentially, it's a multi-colored outer garment
that never needs washing. I saw one hanging in a shop window the other
day, and, boy, did it look fine. In fact, it was even blinding, in its way.

DEVELOPMENT SOUGHT OUT TO STUDY THE ALLEY SCIENTIFICALLY.

Izetta would stand all day in the alley, always in the window, and comb her long hair, she had very long hair, hair that was hundreds, no millions, of years old. It was long and complex and sometimes braided and sometimes flat-ironed. She would stand in the doorway wearing hardly anything at all, it depended on the time of day, whether it was a corset, or more like a lace bra, or more like a sheer French slip. Her immodesty made Mr. Jones uncomfortable. There was nobody like him, nobody as upstanding. He would never walk in the alley, if he could avoid it. Not even in full sun. There was a patch of grass there too, enough to scatter birdseed in. Izetta wished she had a better voice because she would sing, if she could, to the gray and brown wrens that pecked there, gently tweezing what they could out of the only grass in the alley. They especially loved to be there after a brief downpour of rain. The developer, a young international architect, didn't know what to do with this scene, for he was particularly coarse, had coarse tastes in everything: big blocks of taste, all squares and huge numbers; rarely the exception, rarely the finer thing. He did not like fruit, or fruit trees, that's for certain. All fruit was a poison to development, although fruit was not, in fact, a poison to itself. Development's only one exception being a waxy red apple, or maybe an oversized naval orange. The architect didn't have a kind heart, not like Izetta, who wanted to please, who wanted a better voice just so she could sing down the alley to the wrens. Izetta who wanted to cure the whole world of its disease, its toxic lung and silver death, its rusted particles, its ancient membrane, its bald-faced lies, its suffering, its selling itself down the river, its stiff-knees, its stiff-neck, its cancer, its war, its coups, its sowing of its wild oats, its never fixing what it broke, its loneliness. She wanted to install rooftop gardens on all the roofs, where we could grow roma tomatoes and cherry tomatoes and okra and rice and wild barleygrass and rutabaga and stomp out all the grabbing and corruption. Izetta wanted to cancel out this version of the world in particular, the one where you better watch your back, or you better watch your purse, or your buckles, or your jewelry, where you better eat or be eaten, take first or be taken, be the first to act like an asshole. She made me feel that there was no better man than me, person than I. Why didn't all her visitors, including Mr. Jones, not see her kind heart? Or listen to what she had to say? The problem with you Mr. Jones, says Samantha, while they are seated around Izetta's dinner table, is that you used to be a do-gooder, putting others before yourself. It has been a good meal, the lamps are turned down, and there is warmth in the air. Lord Burlington is a little bit embarrassed because Samantha can be a bit harsh when she's overdone it on the gooseberry wine. Her beautiful index finger is pointed straight at Mr. Jones's forehead. And so you gave and you gave, Jones, and you gave from the heart, and you gave, thinking you were going to make the world better. You signed petitions. You went to protests. You are articulated your suffering and those of others. But the world didn't give you exactly what you wanted and all the physical comforts and love and everything else you wanted, and so you just flipped out and became totally self-interested. But I don't buy it. No one just *becomes* self-interested, right? she asks. I had put so much faith in Mr. Jones, but this conversation made me suspicious. Was Mr. Jones only good for sport? For offering a compliment on a new gooseberry coat?

UNDERSTANDING sought out to study THE FLAT EARTH scientifically.

Are you through with your water yet, Izetta? The Mysterious Adolpho asked. I still have this love letter I would like to read to you:

> And there is sport and there is a kind heart, if only you would let it in. I asked and it was answered, but I was waiting by the window. They said that? Well, asked and answered. But heaven is a project. You were standing by the bedside table looking morose, fumbling around for your keys in the dark, when I first saw you. When I first saw you it was dark. It was dark when I first saw you. When we broke up, I instantly turned nine, or, what I meant to say was that when we broke up I instantly turned nice. I wrote nice first. And then I lied. I ate you all up. You were better that way. And the earth rumbles. It loses control because of how fast you have to go. And you have to go fast to get there. In the house, on the earth, in a tree, and there were things growing everywhere. And you have to grow up, you really do, because if you don't grow up then you get haunted real fast and there is a lot of tea in the world after all, and that is all they talk about in schools these days, but I believed every word you said. Every word you said was true. I sat on my hands. I had to find a way in the door. A cloudy day.

In the alley, the Mysterious Adolpho sat on his hands, mumbled to himself, and sighed. There is no one in the doorway. You have fast feet, Izetta,

Adolpho thinks. But this is in no way true. What I was thinking was not true. There is a rooftop garden on the roof of one of the buildings in the alley. Turnips and rutabagas and parsnip, edible weeds of every kind, grow in the rooftop garden. You are just not allowed to eat in the garden with your hands on *some* days, Adolpho says, not *every* day. But you do have to watch how often you eat there or you will be eaten, that's for sure. Why, one time, I was lying on the ground in the garden, and you were a gourmet chef, Izetta. Do you remember that? Izetta sighs. The Mysterious Adolpho sighs and looks at the love letter. He begins to read again:

The whole world has cancer. It is a nightmare and you'd better watch your back. It is morning in the rest of the world and there is nothing to do. But this is decided quickly and by better thinkers than me. Therefore, it is no surprise that I have nothing to do. Therefore, it has to do with my childhood, with the way I was brought up. It was in the olden days, a succession of days, of diseases, of finding out exactly how one was supposed to stand by the window, what shape to take, how to wave one's hands. You were watching the world go by from your window.

PRISON SOUGHT OUT TO STUDY THE EVER-CHANGING BODY SCIENTIFICALLY.

Prison was stuck again, in cement, in rotten smells and rotten cake and dirty clothes, and suffering from want, and bad air, and then he seemed like he could've died, for at least the seventh or eighth time. But then he sprang back because prison never goes away. I said, Prison, what's it like to be sick but never die? And he broke the wizened belt from off his blocky, protuberant, crumbling stomach and shrugged. He said, Too confusing to explain—I can't explain anything that's bigger than me, although I know that in the end there's more out there that's bigger than me, than I. Too confusing. I used to remember everything, all the old songs, all the old questions. And in reply, I said, And it's still the same? He said he wanted to go lie down, but I was pushy, so in love with hope, so comfortable in the dark, and I owned a car, and prison was stuck, a stuck system, breeding and bred by other systems, and wanted very much to be an ever-changing body. But then I started to wonder if I was looking at this all wrong. I started to wonder if prison was gaslighting me. Well, he said, you see... everything dissolves...anything dissolves... anything can crumble. Anything can stop existing, perhaps. Everything can get hurt except the mystery itself. The end tree and the beginning one, all the poisons, and the sack full of the alchemist, the excrement and the alchemist, all the old questions, the smaller tree and the bigger tree, the stick belonging to the shepherd and the shepherd itself. It becomes a big maze. I wanted to fall asleep listening to his stories. I was being lulled underground, I was being lulled to root level, to sleep with the turnips and the rutabagas, the potatoes, under the cement block of prison. I knew I was letting myself get distracted. I knew I wasn't asking the right questions. And there was the rain this time of year. It was drizzling into the grates and the open ground. Prison wanted to say, I just need to rest my head for fifteen minutes. But this conflicted with prison's other urge, to be an ever-changing body. If I really told you what it was like, he said, I can't help it, I've got no straight answers for you. Because everything is right in and of and *to* itself, but is either a poison or a benefit to another, and I've lost track of the difference by now. The biggest misery of all is that I can't tell the difference, he said. I couldn't bear it anymore. We were done with our lunch and we had eaten too many clams right off the shell, and I felt sick. I couldn't bear prison's tangled sentences. I thought of explosives alone, I thought of the ever-changing body, how I could wrench it into being here, being where it had refused to be.

THAT WHICH SOUGHT OUT TO STUDY ITS NEIGHBOR'S BODY SCIENTIFICALLY.

You were such a handsome man, Mr. Jones, said Lord Burlington one day, smiling. You were upside down. And this is a perfect day for a hurricane, for the weather. Or rather, for a partner, a helping hand, so to speak, to fall out of the sky. But what I said was true. The red fish was looking at you. The yellow fish was looking at you, too. And it came in ten parts. You are a prisoner. You live in a fish pond on a great estate, and you can't get out. But it is your heart that is in ten pieces. And I just realized that I was on a patch of grass that day. It is all becoming clear. The way the fish swim. The way the birds fly. The way the turnip and rutabaga and parsnip, edible weeds of every kind, grow. But you are too much of this and too little of that and there are all kinds of ideas and colors and emotions and everything else that just swirls around you, and you don't even have to try that hard! But I was sitting on the grass and it all became clear. That is to say, I remembered. An echo. A buzz in my ear. Noise on a grassy meadow. Something great and something small. Something bigger than me in the end. You would have to look up to find something as fragile in nature. And, after all, there are always going to be bigger trees than me, than I, in the forest. It was a spring day, and I sat there looking all around. I wasn't very religious, at that point. I had barely begun to hold my hand out. I put my hand on my heart, and what I found was you. It was in the beginning. We were swimming around. Just the two of us. We were horsedressing, using horsedressing again regularly, participating in complicated rituals that were designed to tell us exactly who was who, who we were. And that is not going to be allowed any more, you know. Not when you are dressing like a goat and getting all messed up. Not when I love you the way I do. I was messing around, dressing like a goat. I sat on a stone, set in a grassy meadow and remembered everything. There was a smile on your lips and in your eyes. You were just beautiful in your ramshackle house. In your woods. Your neck and the collar you wore. And the fish. The whole fish pond. All of Swabia. The eyes. In the middle of the lawn, right next to the pool, sat a gazebo. Or I swear it was a grassy meadow. Running neck and neck, like in a race, but giving away nothing. It is fury, or it makes me furious. And the red fish was swimming around in circles. It is funny how it all worked out in the end. In the end the fish swam, and the water ran, and you ran too, you ran around the room, you and your gooseberry coat, your shepherd's stick. You and your old songs and your patriotic songs and your questions, too. It was impossible to recognize. A feat. A fit. A glorious solution to all of our problems. And finally I have to rest my case, ease my heart, plant my shepard's stick in the ground, once and for all.

THE HURRICANE SOUGHT OUT TO STUDY THE WAY THINGS WERE DESIGNED SCIENTIFICALLY.

This hurricane was not like the others, she was special, there was no other hurricane like her. Her body was made of pure thermal healing waters—not water rife with decay, with the color of decay, decay hanging off its sprays like old laundry, like molding trash, like rotting walnut shells, like decadence or croaking or a bad exhalation or a bad shade of green or blue or death or corruption or old songs. Or muddy shoes in your laundry basket. Or a bad mole on your thigh, or a bad needle, or cancer. God knows the whole world has cancer. God knows it's easy to think something that isn't true. It's eat or be eaten. The color of decay means you've got to watch your back, or your purse, or your purpose. You've got to fight to breathe. There is nothing in decaying water that is not the color of decay, and there is no decay that doesn't come from a poison. This hurricane, however, was named Esmeralda because she was beautiful and she had a father and she was pure weather. Her father was Mr. Jones. Esmeralda was a hurricane and Mr. Jones was her father. Mr. Jones had a daughter and her name was Esmeralda and she was a hurricane. Esmeralda was a hurricane and her body was made of water, the purest kind. Mr. Jones, because there was no one like him, because of his quality of imagination, was the only one among us who could give birth to a hurricane. But he didn't birth her alone. (We've figured out that the male principle is not enough on its own to bring about creation.) His daughter, Esmeralda, had been rocked in the baths of Swabia, in the deepest springs. Where all the waterlilies were beautiful and led secret communal lives. This hurricane was pure, and a good kind of blue, and carried blessings bestowed by the most peaceful of fish, especially the yellow ones, and the echoes and fragrances of the biggest and the smallest trees. This hurricane, Esmeralda, knew the sound of your beloved jangling his or her keys in the dark when he or she returned home at night. And furthermore, it was because of the existence of this hurricane that everything would come to look exactly like itself, be exactly like itself, exactly like it should, and it was because of this hurricane that we now had enough popular literature in circulation that told us we each had to be our own best friend, we each had to believe that we were somebody, even if we were walking down the street in something as paltry and threadbare (or as regal and high-class, depending on the store) as a gooseberry coat. Because we couldn't do greater violence to ourselves than to make ourselves feel ashamed for being who we were. When Esmeralda was old enough she decided to give the people a show. It was her way of telling the truth. It was a good time to do this because the world was feeling like an afterthought and it was getting harder and harder and more dangerous to be that which you were supposed to be in the first place. The hurricane alighted on a paper mill and took stock of her environment, the firmament, the heavens, the grass beneath her, the pig and the cow in the far corner of the field. Esmeralda had a kind heart because she had worked for it despite adversity. And it was from this kind, clear heart, and from her thermal waters, that she could study the design of things scientifically. She tried to make everyone spin into her centers of gravity. It was her way of granting new vision. It was her way of preparing us for the new world. She told everyone that everything was free and independent, yet mutually dependent, and that there were two worlds existing at once: an invisible side and a material side. This had disappointed the crowds that had gathered at her feet, wearing canvas shoes and bathing suits, drinking her in like she was a waterfall, a remote treasure in a forest, a good vintage, a good view, a plum among the dust. She decided to try a more mainstream approach in order to reach as many people as possible. Her voice ricocheted as she glided confidently down the side of the paper mill, little drops of water peeling out everywhere. First it was quiet and then she sang. *I picked you out, I shook you up, and turned you around. Turned you into someone new.* Hurricanes aren't funny! Was Esmeralda willingly bringing shame on herself, or was she a genius at showing people who they were—simply mirroring them back to themselves? But she had made her father proud, and as I said, I was already beginning to wonder if I trusted him as much as I used to.

THE ALCHEMIST SOUGHT OUT TO STUDY THE WATERLILY SCIENTIFICALLY.

Placing bets on the odds of creating a world bigger than one's self would eventually lead Mr. Jones into a heap of trouble. But it begins to be a little harder to become that which you are supposed to become in the first place. Supposed to become? What? Like a waterlily? asked Mr. Jones, attempting irony. For instance, look at Izetta, she does nothing at all but stand around in the alley, and what kind of becoming is that? But her clothes are multi-colored and very fashionable, added Esmeralda, Mr. Jones's daughter. When she bothers to wear them, huffed Mr. Jones. Still, the fish in the fish pond would, of course, in time, become multi-colored too. All those fish, thinks Mr. Jones. Where do the colors come from? And there were the fish at the bottom of Lord Burlington's swimming pool to contend with too. Still, things were getting better and better and things were getting worse and worse and, after a while, it all felt a bit like standing naked at the edge of a cold, harsh, and indifferent void with no multi-colored outer garment to wear and nothing good to eat, and yet, in the end, still having to find romance when and where it wanted to be found, or not at all. Mr. Jones sang his daughter Esmeralda an old song to help her fall asleep. The song pleased her and she went on to lead a very happy life filled with many pleasant and varied and restorative dreams, even though she did some-times dream that she lived all alone and that the neighbors were loathsome and did horrible things at night or that their friends who came over to visit did horrible things at night or that there were people in the neighborhood who were not very pleasant and did horrible things at night. But, by then, it was getting late, and Mr. Jones remembered that he had to write a quick message to Dr. Honorable. Dr. Honorable had planned to take his students from the Swabian Medical College on a field trip. First they were going to view a grassy meadow, and then they were going to visit Mr. Jones and, they hoped, see the hurricane. Mr. Jones, however, wanted to cancel the field trip. He was just not up for visitors that day. Mr. Jones wrote out his cancellation message on a very pretty picture postcard of the Swabian coast and put it in the mail. He was pleased. It was the first time in a long while that he had engaged the world, communicated what he wanted, directly. And this must be what it means when they say, pushing up daisies! thought Jones. And, hey, like it says in the song: *I was working as a waitress in a cocktail bar, that much is true. But even then I knew I'd find a much better place...*

THE CONSCIENCE OF THE WORLD SOUGHT OUT TO STUDY ACTUAL OBJECTS SCIENTIFICALLY.

Strictly speaking the conscience of the world was not an aristocrat, nor did he have aristocratic leanings, and people knew that. He was hunched over in an old suit, a cringing horsehair jacket he had purchased from a thrift store in the village with a few dimes and pennies. It was the good kind of dark blue, although a little gloomy. The conscience of the world dressed nothing like Mr. Jones. Mr. Jones was always mistaken for being wealthier than he actually was. Or some kind of hero from a European war, like a decorated lieutenant of the calvary, a Swabian commander, with brilliantly braided front pockets, a figure of calm and certitude. Perhaps it was his gait. Or the way he refused to eat with his bare hands, the directions he glanced in when he ate. People projected onto Mr. Jones surefire convictions of all kinds. Their relationship to him was wonderfully eccentric. Or rather, it wasn't. Because Mr. Jones was and had always been wonderfully attractive to women. He was well groomed, with his dyed hair combed straight back (or was it naturally dark?). And these impressions are not merely mine, I promise you. When he was young he thought he could recreate the world. Offer people real cures, solutions, health food regimens, alternatives to insecticides. But he was eventually to learn that these causes were not his to take up; they belonged to the conscience of the world. The conscience of the world traveled far, hopping on trains and so forth, to get to a hill in the north woods of Europe. The hill was very high up in the clouds and from its vantage point the conscience of the world could survey a plenitude of actual objects near and far. There were many objects to see, trace, or hold; yachts, for example, handrails, things cut out of wood or silver (which was less gaudy than gold). And there was more. All the law firms in Dalmatia or Salmatia. European ruins. The great cultural monuments. Fish ponds growing stinking mosses, and stinking tars in alleyways. Newspapers and things cut out of newspapers. Combs. Garlic. Birds, train terminals, amazing things. Gothic castles. Dim brains. Light. The economy. Wonderful and disturbing stuff. Board chairmen. Plasterboard. Viewless corridors. Pharmaceuticals. CEO's. Antidotes. All sorts of structures with impressive intent. Great cultural monuments. Glassware. Colorless sheets of industrial plate glass. Cozy white sofas. In fact, many things made of white cylindrical shapes. Plus hob-tread metal spiral stairways. Ramps. Bare faces shaved with razors. Hurricanes. Cider. The rose at the back of the house. Wild barleygrass. Rooftop gardens and songs of miraculous sensitivity. Songs that made you feel better because they articulated your suffering. The conscience of the world longed so deeply for a clean and pure and just future! He wanted to remake the world, and with more music and without all the hobbling and begging and fighting. Could you imagine? A whole world made of honest materials. Honest people. The Truth! Really! Fires lit in the fireplaces. Tropical green leaves festooning people's clothes. And no more detestable architecture! The conscience of the world was our chief hope. But Mr. Jones, although he wouldn't necessarily let on, felt a little emasculated by comparison. Without a blush he said to me, drinking a soda and then crushing the aluminum in his bare hands, the problems, *all* of them, are on their way to being solved, I assure you.

NOURISHMENT sought out to study THE VACUOUS WORLD scientifically.

The five years we have had have been such good times. I still love you. But now I think it's time I lived my life on my own. I guess it's just what I must do... sang Mr. Jones. It had been that kind of day. The ocean roared. There was love on the horizon. But something is wrong here, sighed Mr. Jones. I felt much stronger when I was alive. I feel I was, in fact, most perfect before I was dead. Why, I was a handsome man, women apparently adored me, and I really ought to get myself back to that level of conditioning before I suffer even one more humiliating setback. I loved working with Mr. Jones, you know. I really did, said nourishment one day, musing out loud. He was so receptive, and intuitively so. I was not at all happy the first time I heard that he was dead. That happened a long time ago, though. And I get bored of my memories. Why, I remember the day well. I was sitting on the grassy meadow. I was happily thinking of barleygrass and of beneficial poisons and of multi-colored fish and fish ponds and of memories. The delicious contents of my picnic basket. I have no memory, you see. But it is a heavy metal, gentlemen. And mucous and poison. And it dissolves in the blood, explains Dr. Honorable. Dr. Honorable has taken his students from the Swabian Medical College on a field trip. No, no, that's not the fish pond, explains Dr. Honorable. That's a pool of blood, and Mr. Jones is dead. Why, she was just a little whirlpool, at first, says Mr. Jones, and now she's all grown up. Why, it's just the living end. Later it began to rain, and Esmeralda turned out to be a delightful and competent hurricane hostess, if ever there was one, says nourishment dreamily. Such delicious horsesauce. And turnips. And tea. Perfect for a rainy afternoon. But you should have seen

Mr. Jones in life. He was a very handsome man, continues Dr. Honorable, shifting his students' attention away from the grassy meadow and to the rolling Swabian hills. And when it is raining, and when the tops of the trees are very green, you can, sometimes, get a sense of the whole situation, see the big picture, so to speak, see how it all stands right now. Though, of course, it can, at first, be somewhat off-putting. And did you catch the pushing up daisies reference? Did you get that Mr. Jones was dead? Esmeralda was standing on a grassy meadow all covered in gooseberry, or rather, wearing a multi-colored gooseberry coat, sighs nourishment again. She looked beautiful. And Mr. Jones, was there too. It is on account of the weather, ladies and gentlemen, says Dr. Honorable. The hurricanes, the rain, the lush green grass on the meadow, and to think that this is the way it is going to be for all eternity. Why, in the end, it is impossible for one to deny what one knows. I mean look at this. Dr. Honorable points his finger to the top of a very green tree. Still, the true nature of things does sometimes slip the mind and that, of course, can lead to all kinds of complications, or rather, distractions. Something like a lead foot, or a compass, or a bee-sting, if you will. And Mr. Jones actually never even knew what hit him. He never even knew, not really. And, ladies and gentlemen, to think, they say it is a vacuous world!

THE PATIENT SOUGHT OUT TO STUDY HIS CHIEF HOPE SCIENTIFICALLY.

It had been a long time since the patient had been able to keep down a good meal. Ever since the hurricane and the very tragic death of his good friend and teacher Mr. Jones, he had not been able to eat spicy foods, or things reeking of garlic. Even the crystal clear, purgative, healing waters of Swabia could not give him the lift he had been wanting. He was despondent. He ate vegetable mush. He tried insoles. Nothing, no pain relief. He decided to hire a decorator. This was his chief hope. Maybe if he let more tropical green into the house, paint the walls, add small potted fan palms that reacted to the atmosphere with the greatest sensitivity. Not to be outdone, he hired the most famous decorator of the day. And the decorator began to festoon the plasterboard walls with shimmering little sweet things; he tossed out the requisite white couch, added coziness and color. Don't worry, the decorator said to the patient. If your demand is to be at home in your time and place, this will take a lot of decorating, but then rest assured, we will use honest materials, let in the light. Be assured, the problem is on the way to being solved. But the decorator had other things on his mind, and he slipped up. This is how it happened. He hired men to paint the hallway yellow; he recommended halogen lamps, sheets of industrial plate glass. Because, even though his intentions were good, his thoughts were really and truly elsewhere. He was tired of being lonely. He wanted a community of two. And there was that woman in the alley. A shimmering little sweet thing standing in the doorway, holding a long spoon, wearing very little. He had heard her name was Izetta. A beautiful name, not too gaudy. He had heard she had a thing for odd-lot intellectuals. And he thought about all the ways he could impress her with his list of eccentric hobbies: writings on comets, the year 1897, the birds of the north woods of Europe, identifying edible weeds, growing tomatoes and mustard greens on a rooftop garden. She was wearing yellow that day, gauzy and not too gold, but sheer enough to see her heart pulsing real, vibrant blood down into her bare feet. Or was she wearing a cream-colored slip? She was a force of nature, how she clamped the empty spoon, looked at him with such diffident green eyes. Was this love? And if it was, then why had the decorator failed the patient by suggesting, of all things, a halogen lamp in front of a plate-glass window? Wasn't love supposed to be a curative? Wasn't it supposed to be an end to all war? A chief hope? *The* chief hope? *The heart of the world must keep beating or else we are all doomed.* He kicked a stone down the alley. Saw her from a distance, casting a shadow onto the undisturbed concrete. It was said she had no desire to cause another pain. Did he need to change his style of facial hair? Grow a mustache? What was the highest degree of perfection man was capable of achieving?

THE GLASS BOX SOUGHT OUT TO STUDY ODD-LOT INTELLECTUALS SCIENTIFICALLY.

It was remorse, Mr. Jones said, buyer's remorse. But that was the way things always were with Mr. Jones at that time. Izetta was standing in the alley. She was wearing a new outfit. A multi-colored gooseberry coat, shoes, hat, galoshes, a cane, and a candle. It was a condition. Seeing red. And the story begins, here and there. It begins in the way things often begin, here and there. But the odd-lot intellectuals always return. Lousy odd-lot intellectuals, minding their ways, attaching themselves methodically to the dreams and ideas of their countrymen. But there is no way to combine the two things, Mr. Jones sighs. Concrete, glass, and steel—the key ingredients for a glass box—just do not mix and match well with my geraniums. But the glass box is not so easily repressed. The glass box looks at Mr. Jones sternly and says, there is a useless way about you, mister. You are failing to notice what you notice. Half the time, you are gazing uselessly, daydreaming, looking at the great blue sky and demanding to be a part of your time, demanding to be at home in your time without doing a damned thing about it. And that's the one thing an odd-lot intellectual never does. The one thing a human being cannot get away with, if they hope to succeed in the world, that is. And there you go again. Unbelievable! Mr. Jones was, in fact, gazing, so to speak. This is getting to be exasperating! And you can just hear the odd-lot intellectuals laughing, mister. And they too are wearing their gooseberry finest, their coats and galoshes and walking sticks, and they too are marching to the beat of their own drummers. It is the war all over again, but as the saying goes, war is a fucking bore so get over it already, at least when there are glass boxes to build. And there are many,

many glass boxes to build! Then the glass box laughs. It is amusing to try and reason with Mr. Jones. For instance, mister, have you ever really appreciated what a marvelous part I have played in the interesting and continuously unfolding drama of the world? But that's a cliché, Mr. Jones screams. He is sitting in his den, holding the fire, putting the flame first to one side of his mouth and then to the other. That is the beaten path! Well, Jones, you are a spunky debater today, but please remember that the streets are always either lined with gold or glass boxes, never both at the same time. So the choice is yours. But, if you wait too long to decide, I promise: the odd-lot intellectuals will beat you to the punch every time. Now, Mr. Jones has reached the limit of his patience. He is very angry. Why, in my day, exclaims Mr. Jones, people walked from place to place. Why, my grandfather dressed in a gooseberry coat and hat and walked for miles in every type of weather. Why, in my day, the streets were lined with gold, and gold could turn a man just like that.

THE MAN WHO HAD TRUE IDEAS SOUGHT OUT TO STUDY THE MAN WHO HAD FALSE IDEAS SCIENTIFICALLY.

Or, I should say, I sought out to study you scientifically. But you didn't let me. You had your mind on other things. Writings on comets, for example, false cures (or the wracking up of medical bills), ham radios, architecture, attempting to predict hurricanes (which, again, you had done poorly—as was evidenced by the hounding winds of Esmeralda and the way she woke up all of Swabia one morning, singing). And war is so goddammed fucking boring. And your war. And your personal war. And your domestic war, and your international one. And your great war is so fucking boring. And so I was forced to do something I had not intended. I had to build an image box. That's right, an image box. You said it didn't exist. But you had nothing but false ideas. You dressed in poor, wan shades of blue. The bad kind of blue. You are weak. You are a coward. You are an asshole. And therefore you were wrong as always. And I'll tell you something. I built the image box! It was real, an actual object. And it was redder than the ocean. And more radical. Bigger than the ocean too, and more special, and more great, and made of silver, with clean edges festooned with tropical mauves and greens. When it was complete, it caught the sun in every possible direction, sent spirals of light all the way down the streets, lighting up all the dim alleys in the city. All the birds in the city started to sing so loudly. All the people in the city were drawn to the image box at once. When they looked into it, they saw the part they played in the continuously unfolding drama of the world itself. When rebels looked into the image box they saw spies. Architects saw decorators. And all the law firms in Dalmatia or Salmatia saw the bareness of it all. CEOs saw buckets and buckets of endless all-you-can eat clam shells. All empty and eaten. When you looked into the image box, you saw me. And vice-versa. Was the whole world at war? It's very possible, I thought. And why are we all still so vulnerable? After all, we have perfected glass. We have perfected tomatoes. We have perfected shoes, and hair dye. And You. We have perfected You. You, who wouldn't let me study your false ideas scientifically. And your violence is so goddamned fucking shiteously boring. But even still, I know how you think. You are afraid of me. You are all ego. You are afraid of community. And two-minded too. You always look up when you are hugging your children to make sure that you see me seeing you. You are afraid everything is going to end up like the ruins of Europe. You think everything has progressed since 1897. But you, you prefer detestable architecture, fireless fireplaces, a world swarming with bureaucrats and CEOs and ineffective medicines and just so many lies. You prefer your house on fire. Your food without nutrition. Your food altered in laboratories. Tested on rats. Combined with pigs. Your reaction to this intolerable world is totally inappropriate. You are the intolerable world. It makes my head hurt. And you want to use my own goodness against me. You want to make me look bad by suggesting that I take this image box and donate it to charity, a non-profit? But I won't. I will strap on my big blue boots (the good kind of blue) and give up on all fanfare. Live simply. Be tough but openhearted. Take my wardrobe down to a mere three articles of clothing. Like a gooseberry coat and a pair of sturdy shoes. Plant trees with curative properties and listen to the winds and its many sensitivities. I will head north to the woods of Europe. Drink in the healing waters of Swabia and bathe in the green salts. I will do the work it takes to be at home in my own time. This is what I will do. All because you will not let me study you or let me in on the secret of your false ideas. You do not want to know the truth of why you think the way you do!

The Blue Ox shrugs and sighs. A page of a manifesto—lying right there in the grassy meadow. And her only decision is to let the wind carry it away. Today I prepared for the new world, says Samantha. Samantha is sitting beside the Blue Ox in Lord Burlington's garden, and it is raining a bit, but not so much that they are uncomfortable. The Blue Ox is braiding Samantha's hair and Samantha is braiding the Blue Ox's tail. I think using the word death is simply enough to represent death, Samantha says. Today I said the word death 50 times, over and over again, even when I was doing the stupidest things, like taking a bath, and then I prepared myself for the new world. I can tell you this because you are my good and true friend, and I can tell you anything.

AFTER THE GREAT WAR SOUGHT TO STUDY THE RUINS OF EUROPEAN CIVILIZATION SCIENTIFICALLY.

And emotion. For fixedness becomes this place even better than the worst of us would imagine. We are red. We are as red as the ocean. A fixedness, I say. A fixedness that sets in, that settles into place. And they live in their image boxes. But, pshaw, image box is not even a word. Now, try glass box. There is a word, a phrase, even! And you are born. And there is great strength in the realization that your gooseberry coat can get along by itself, but only if it really wants to. It is too noisy in the country, all the birds sing all the time. You are standing by the edge of the road and trying to be wise. You are trying to grow up and become your own best friend, but there is a spider in the alley, and suddenly you don't trust spiders. In fact, you don't trust anything quite as much as you used to. Silver was perfect, gold was too gaudy. There was smoke and no fire. There were shoes and no feet. There were empty cages, a huge amount of spiral. Of spiral? What they say is the universe's shape. And you are looking for truth in your way. You see, the great war ended some time ago. There were plenty of ashes then, a sort of starting at zero, if you will. The gazebo on fire, a whole world at war. But the universe bemoans the fact that you can't come out and play as often as you'd like to. Yet the universe is indifferent to the way you feel about spiders, and contradictions, and indications, and medicines, and the prevailing winds. And that is in and of itself a type of starting from zero. It was never this way before. You sigh. You stand in the middle of the street and build an image box. No, you have glass, you have perfected glass, and all the while you have been building a variety of glass boxes. No, it is the end this time, and there is a multi-colored coat and a spiral stairway in the alley that would lead all the way to a place you could trust, if given the opportunity, if given half the chance. And the color is gold. No, I said it was silver. You don't listen to me. You don't love me. You never listen to me. Architects love their paper blue, the good kind of blue. They love their silver, their orange and that is why the world is so screwed up. An anchor. A foot in the door. A jovial occasion and a reflection of the way things used to be. After the great war. Great things after the great war. Swabian castles made of paper, verifiable wonderlands, and the possibility of running away from home to join a community of artists, thieves, intellectuals, rebels, spies, hurricanes, and belts, and in the middle of all of this comes a wonderfully eccentric relationship. Odd-lot intellectuals are roaming through Europe. It is a time of dreams—the relationship is wonderfully eccentric—it is the time of the maelstrom, and if you were young, it was wonderful stuff: recreating the world.

THE ARBITRARY SOCIAL AND POLITICAL STRUCTURES SOUGHT OUT TO STUDY AN IDEAL HEALTH REGIMEN SCIENTIFICALLY.

They had heard very good things about balneology, particularly the thermal waters of Swabia. So, they thought they would start there. Apparently, the water of Swabia was so great, even its hurricanes were soothing. Apparently the waters of Swabia were sensitive and miraculous. They could really wake a person up. Make a person feel barrel-chested and great. They could make any kind of flower grow, even the most difficult kinds: white gooseberry flowers with the flavor of lemon and aniseed, orange daisies, tropical green orchids. You could dip your feet into the ocean and feel new approaches to nature, new movements, the foot soles coming to life for the first time. Finally, there were shoes for your feet. And the waters could wash anything clean. After all, the arbitrary social or political structures knew—and had known—what that spot on their coat was and what had caused it. It was a pool of blood, you idiot, anyone could tell you that. It was the rough and tumble of it all. The slap on the back that knocks the wind out, the fear of the spiders in the alley. The great wars. All the detestable architecture. The bare-faced buildings cramping the cities. And the traffic. And the injustice of it all. The injustice of it all. The arbitrary social or political structures wanted to get to Swabia quickly so they invented newspapers, the newspapers gave people a good deal of information, and that made people feel smart (or dumb, or just crowded, depending on one's perspective) and then the idea of newspapers led to the idea of airplanes. The arbitrary social or political structures boarded an airplane made of honest materials and prayed that as they flew over the woods and mountains of Europe, across the train tracks, across the green hills, and over the factories and gray ocean, they would arrive in Europe safely. What they hadn't realized was this: that when they had invented airplanes they had also created what would become the ruins of European civilization, and even more than that, the resulting emergence of CEOs, pharmaceuticals, and devices for pest control, resulting in, inevitably, the Swabian Paper Company. Or paper mill. And the millions of manifestos fluttering in the streets. The Swabian Paper Company tended to harvest trees (cut them down with hacksaws), making the land buzz materialistically, making the land saw-toothed and loud, and causing people to have many respiratory complaints. And these paper companies had to bleach the pulp and, therefore, had to use the waters of Swabia while also dumping pletchy effluvium and artificial contaminants and barely moving grease back into these waters. The waters were struck with egregious waste; clogged and re-clogged with brown muck. Tom Terrific, The Acting Mayor of All Swabia, thinks about this sitting under a tree. He thinks often about mud and water. He thinks he has figured it all out. *Amnesty is a precondition for the war machine. Aloe vera. The beneficial effect of a hurricane. I will head to the ocean and have a rest. There is nothing like a good foot rub to help you take your place in history.* And so many years ago the arbitrary social and political structures had invented airplanes, but by the time that they had arrived in Swabia, hoping to take in the healing balms, the vapors, the naturally occurring eucalyptus oils, the waters of various temperatures and temperaments, what they found was nothing but emptiness. Swabia was empty, you see. The ocean was so big and empty that it had vanished. Tourist traps. Seagulls. Bathers by the sea in droves. Seals barking for fish. Stinking harbors. Plutocrats, board chairman, CEOs, pharmaceuticals, commissioners and college presidents, and all the clam shells you could think of. Ladies hired to throw ice water on your chest and give you a bracing slap across the mouth. So much red by the ocean. So much red in the ocean. What do we do now? they thought. Eat a mush of pure vegetables? Avoid garlic? Invent curatives for ancient pathologies? We want to be better than we are. But are or aren't such things possible? They were disillusioned, and tired. Plus their mind was elsewhere. Tropical green. The parrots on the telephone poles. And the image box was spotlighting the girl in the alleyway. The way it had lit up her yellow dress and made it look like gold, but not too gaudy. Or just the same color as… Let us relax here on the beach, they thought, and think of things far away. After all, the young will soon inherit the earth. And they will want to recreate the world. Only timidly imitate old models. Let us rest now, for they are our chief hope.

OUR CHIEF HOPE SOUGHT OUT TO STUDY YOUNG INTERNATIONAL ARCHITECTS SCIENTIFICALLY.

You are roaming the seas to nowhere, you know. At least that's what Samantha said to a passing hurricane one fine spring day when there was no one home at Mr. Jones's house and there was no spider to trust and no love to be found anywhere on the grassy meadow. But you are so gruesome in your way, Spider. And Samantha laughs. She has found a way to laugh after all the years. And there are plenty of spiders, and Jones rubs his hands together in a kind of anticipation. The feast is going to be marvelous. There will be jugglers there and clowns, and odd-lot intellectuals, too. But you can never truly identify a glass box solely from the materials it is made from. Sure, certainly, glass and steel, but so much more. And they said a glass box casts no shadows. Hadn't you heard? And your run-of-the-mill odd-lot intellectual shies away from the possibility of timidly imitated European models every time, i.e., the truth. The glass box is turning itself on its head. The glass box is suddenly turning into something I didn't expect. And the truth stands on one side connected, in this case, by glass. And the non-truth, or desertion, or lies, stands on the other side, like a flame or a suit of armor. Mr. Jones rubs one side of his face with fire, and the other side with the truth. He wants you to be just like him in the end. But I am like him, screams Mr. Jones. In fact, I was born that way, he sighs. He is in the waiting room and there is someone's half-eaten lunch on the chair right next to him. He was born a spy, in an agency, with a helmet on, by the burning ashes that the great war left in its wake. It is a time for feasting, for celebration, for laughing, for foaming at the mouth, and then you have to sing yourself a lullaby, say goodbye to the way things were before you even think about approaching the truth in the alleyway. But after 1945, our plutocrats, our designers of bare-faced glass boxes, our young international architects came out of time. They rebelled against the notion of dishonesty, of cowardice, of solutions, of the possibility of abandonment as a viable way out. Thus, step right up. Thus, in this tent we have a cold, a common cold, and the way things are. In other words, the truth is here, and over there is the non-truth, or lies, or rather, the maelstrom, strictly speaking, that is. And please don't apologize to the spider in the alley. The spider let itself in with its keys. The keys no one even knew the spider had. The spider has keys and shares them with whomever and whatever it meets in the alley, whenever it feels like it, that is. And all the Mysterious Adolpho had to do was listen to the song. The maelstrom would come regardless of whatever one trusted, regardless of whatever one had to say, and the only recourse would be a commune, a spiritual movement, a radical approach to art in all its forms. And this because I said so, and this because you said so, and this because of the bare-faced glass boxes they have bought, and not because of a health food regimen consisting solely of fresh vegetable mush after all.

THE ANIMALS AND FRUITS SOUGHT OUT TO STUDY FOOD SCIENTIFICALLY.

There were countless varieties of animals and fruits in the world, and of all colors and shapes, full of different textures, seeds, smells and consistencies. Too many to document. Like the fish at the very bottom of the sea. Like all of Lord Burlington's financial holdings, which were complex and diversified to the point of indecipherability. The Swabian Paper Company, for example, also had agricultural interests. Tobacco. Horsetomatoes. Therefore this attempt at complete documentation was indeed a potentially infinite undertaking, and one that Mr. Jones had prophesized about back when we were in college and I was still thinking I looked smart in my gooseberry coat and hat and cane and was fantasizing about making my own plum cognac grown from plum vinegar, made in my own secret home laboratory. Man, that coat was loud! Mr. Jones was dead again (was this the sixth time? the seventh?). I asked him, Mr. Jones, what's it like? He said, tossing a clean ball of fire around in his hands, scrubbing his perfectly shaved chin (that the ladies used to love) with something that resembled sandpaper (but wasn't), Well, different every time, really. This time I'm going to try dying again better. I'm thinking of planting a vegetable garden. Eating pure vegetable mush. Avoiding garlic. Avoiding conflict. Being my own best friend. Buying some fruit trees. I was thinking of the standard varieties: a sweet lemon, a giant kumquat, a pomegranate, an orange, a tropical green, and of course an evergreen. And roma tomatoes. I asked him what he thought his cause of death had been this last time around. He told me that he hadn't been sure entirely. It could have been a war or a bad remedy, but it didn't have anything to do with the body, exactly. It hadn't been something that the body itself had produced, exactly. The body is itself perfect. But of course there was the existence of poison. And poison was really real. Poison in the air and in the lake. Poison in our clothes. Poison in our money, our answering machines. But he looked bored as he watered his black box, or knife container, or symptom machine, or ventilator. This made him look very mysterious and smart all over again. He said that poison was actually a very narrow topic of conversation. Our only poisons come from that which we eat or consume (as in purchase, invent, buy, or collect). He was poking one of his cheeks. Again he looked very intelligent and powerfully unknowable. He said we must never forget the toxins in our cultural productions—what we purchase when we go to the movies, the toxins in the overhead lamps, the sheet metal, the conversations, the books, the fabrics, bleak, all of it, he said, but full of potential. He said to remember that *poison is not poison to itself.* We were standing in the back of Lord Burlington's estate. We were standing in a wide-open field with a great view. We were standing in a sea of gravy. The animals and fruits of all varieties and shapes agreed with Mr. Jones. He was good that way. Was it true, then, that if I eat a plum, or a peach, then I will begin to think like one? Was it true that if the Blue Ox ate some wild green barleygrasses, or the husks of gooseberry branches, then she would begin to think like them? The Blue Ox answered my question. She said, *my body, after all, is land, and my soul is elemental.* Was it true that if a lion gnawed on a fine pair of antlers, electric and alive with all the knowledge of the universe, that the lion would have a mind full of such qualities? The animals and fruits were riddled with such questions, day and night, and therefore sought to study food because nothing is poison to itself any more than food is food to itself. And that which might not be poisonous to us might be poisonous to them. Mr. Jones interrupted and said, Hey buddy, mister, Tom Terrific, Pal-O-Mine, friend, cat, etc., show me your grief. I might know how to mend it. I scoffed at Mr. Jones and got up off the porch. He was tending to his snap peas. He said they tasted sweet but not sugary. Now this is how a snap pea is really supposed to taste, said Mr. Jones.

THE DIET CONSISTING OF A MUSH OF FRESH VEGETABLES SOUGHT TO STUDY TROPICAL GREEN SCIENTIFICALLY.

And this, of course, took place in the lovely land of Swabia a long, long time ago. He makes mention of Swabia before he goes to bed. It is the paper mill he remembers best. A house on the corner. A hill by the lake next to the mill. And there is a rapid degradation of memory after that. The ways in which Mr. Jones does and does not remember anything at all. To be honest, I have never been to the coast of Swabia, have never seen its shores, The Mysterious Adolpho says. I have never been to the coast of Swabia and sat in its famous curative waters, rested in its tropical green. But odd-lot intellectuals. It never stopped odd-lot intellectuals before. You know the kind I mean. The ones running around Europe. Odd-lot. An odd-lot, I say. And this is Swabia, and that is Swabia, or at least Swabian thinking, or at least the thinking of the paper mill, the factory, the glass box, the spider, the truth on this side and on that. I am bored, and I am boring. And I am going to Swabia this spring and then again in the summer so I will feel less bored and be less boring, Mr. Jones said to The Mysterious Adolpho one day. I am dead and a Swabian vacation is just the thing for me. I have been looking at the universe all wrong. It doesn't begin and it doesn't end. It is a spiral! Lord Burlington, you are back. And the children sing a song. And Lord Burlington is indeed back. But if I go to the coast of Swabia on vacation I will have to sit, says Mr. Jones, and listen to Lord Burlington and his millions and millions of lies. I will have to take myself out of this patch of grass I have been lying around in for the longest time and cool my heels and become a real European intellectual. There is a back road into deepest Swabia that only Lord Burlington knows about. He knows the secrets of the paper mill and glass boxes and silver and health food regimens, but after 1945 it all began to change. He hiked the Swabian hills. He got a haircut. He began to love himself madly all over again, and it was like he was the universe, and it was like he was reborn. But he wasn't a spiral. But I am Swabia all over again, recreated, so to speak. And it *is* strange, Lord Burlington says. I was thinking of a flower, a particular flower I used to love, and all I could see were daisies, millions and millions of them. This is funny and ironic because Mr. Jones just loves daisies. And he has been waiting for an opportunity to one-up Lord Burlington all night. The Swabian coast. The European artist, what a dazzling figure! And in the end there is disease and there is a cost to the various remedies one may seek. The cost of quality healthcare in Swabia is just too damned high. And each and every Swabian citizen has been overcharged for generations. But a Swabian should know better. An authentic Swabian citizen would hold each and every lie up to the fire and give each and every one of them exactly what it deserves. It's the voice in the wilderness that's never heard, though, sighs Mr. Jones. Swabia, if you will. Swabia, and thanks for reminding me, Jones, Lord Burlington says, I'd forgotten all about that story. My trip to Swabia began rather unexpectedly. I was holding court with a group of odd-lot intellectuals, the kind, incidentally, that one used to see roaming about Europe during those days...

THE BOOKISH PHYSICIAN SOUGHT OUT TO STUDY THE HIGHLY FRUITFUL PHASE OF HIS LIFE SCIENTIFICALLY.

He was lounging by the fish pond on Lord Burlington's estate. There was a hill and a cut lawn that ranged beyond where the eye could see. The sky was clear and open that day, and the bookish physician was sipping on a red straw and throwing darts. Cecil was a big fan of archery. The physician's previous experiment had been a success: on Lord Burlington's avid recommendation he had, for four weeks, consumed nothing but the infamous healing thermal waters of Swabia. He had drunk them hot, cold, and at room temperature. He had bathed in Swabian ice cubes and intrepidly steamed his face and sinuses with their many good and powerful qualities. And now he felt robust and barrel-chested and even a little smug. He felt like two people living harmoniously in one body. Which was remarkable, because who really does not war constantly with oneself/themselves and who is not constantly of two minds, really, when you really stop to think about it (already a paradox in itself, you thinking of yourself, said Cecil, brushing a rabbit hair off of his velvet coat. No, he said, it's not a coat, it's a goddamned jacket. His dart had missed its mark.). The physician had never felt better in his life. Nor more sensual either, a lilt was present in every syllable he pronounced. He was even thinking of approaching the woman in the alley, the one who dressed so sensitively, so provocatively, in a lace dress, a little like a Victorian undergarment, or a peach-colored slip. Her strap falling off her shoulder. Her bare feet. A piece of hair falling over her ear. Her unified heart. And the way she looked so vulnerable and sad and speechless. The physician said, Hey, Burlington, I see you are looking slowly at your hands. Is there something that you need me to diagnose?

Lord Burlington simply laughed. You said the same thing to me yesterday, when I was tweezing my mustache. Really, Dr. Honorable, you ought to get your mind off of business. I am merely looking at the silver dime in my hand. I am hoping to throw it into my fish pond and make a wish with it. But I have read the stars first, or have had someone read them for me, and today is not the day. Neither Lord Burlington, nor Cecil, nor Dr. Honorable could decide, once again, whether it was or was not the end of the world. And once again Lord Burlington did not make a wish. That's what happens when you sit on things for too long. And before you know it, it's the dead men who rule everything. And all of Europe and elsewhere is in ruins. And war and its effects are no longer interesting topics of art or conversation. But it is good we are no longer entertained by war, right Honorable, man? said Cecil, snapping the elastic band of his swimming trunks. Feeling spontaneous, and in a very successful stage of his life, the physician took one more sip of lukewarm Swabian water. It tasted somewhat salty but not too salty. Then he bounded up out of his beach chair, and proclaimed, We should tear the pages out of some *undead* man's book! The rainbow of fish in the fish pond burbled the water and sent little pockets of air to the surface. They swam in and out of the spidery green moss, tried to not to eat the poisons, the poisons in the air, the water, the plants, the soil, the mercury or lead in the coins of Lord Burlington's previous wishes. What is a balm to us can be a poison to them, said Cecil, grabbing for a custard-colored cloth napkin. And is everyone wearing sun protection? If we're not careful even the crystalline waters of Swabia can become stagnant and unmerciful and full of terrible grease and grime, he added. The bookish physician did not listen to Cecil, nor to Lord Burlington, nor to the fish. He was feeling so pleasant and was learning how not to listen. It takes great skill to learn when to listen, to use one's attentions selectively. Think of all the distractions and lies. One must have this skill in order to simply enjoy this most successful and healthy time in one's life.

THAT WHICH IS NOT POISONOUS TO THEM
ATTEMPTED TO SCIENTIFICALLY STUDY THAT WHICH IS POISONOUS TO US.

It began in an image-box. You know what I mean? Detrimental, or rather, image-boxes are sometimes detrimental. As if the whole world depended on them. And you were in your clothes, and by that I mean to say that you were dressed. But this was the whole world. A system. Each day, depending on the amount of dimes that one or more of them possessed. You mean to say that Mr. Jones possessed a dime? I meant to say that Mr. Jones held a dime in his hand, but it looked like a big, delicious peach. And it was not the end of the world. It was, simply, by all accounts, the end of the world. And image-boxes. Jones, did I tell you about image-boxes? What they are capable of producing? The whole concept of image-boxes? Jones drops his hands. He regards himself slowly by staring at his hands. He puts himself, in a sense, out of reach, by staring at his hands, regarding them, though only momentarily. Goddamned gooseberry coat. What was that you said, Jones? Ahem! I'm sorry, Jones, old man, did you say something? Goddamned gooseberry coat, or rather, jacket. It was, in fact, a jacket I was referring to. But Mr. Jones was sensitive, too sensitive perhaps. And then longing for things. There was always plenty of longing for things in those days. But goddamn gooseberry coat! Fit perfectly the last time I tried it on. That's what happens when you wait too long. When you sit on things too long. But, man, that jacket, was nice. Real nice. It was loud, too. Inspired! I remember once. In Swabia. On the coast of Swabia. And you told me, whispered in my ear, that dead men ruled. Dead men ruled. I could swear you shouted that dead men rule. But you were happy then, Jones, were you not?

I mean you had a lot of friends then. I mean your friends used to see you smile. But, from time to time, one is bound to factor in a lot of things that can't be properly accounted for. And, I mean, the coat, baby, the coat: it was loud. That jacket was loud; no, the jacket was out of control. No, that jacket was out of control! And what do you do when you talk to total strangers? How does the encounter make you feel about yourself? And there is poison in the food you eat. In fact, peach pits themselves are totally poisonous. That jacket was out of control. You were certainly out of control and your digestive system was totally out of whack as a result of how out of control you were. Mr. Jones raises his hands. He wants to get a word in, but there is something stuck in his throat. But you are getting very negative here, Esmeralda says. You are by nature very good and wholesome and out of control and you used to be just like a peanut butter and jelly sandwich but that was the past and this is today and there is just no more left to say on the subject of food. I am exhausted. But I could have choked to death just now, marvels Jones. He is holding the peach pit that had been stuck in his throat between his fingers. Goddamn peach was delicious, though. I wish I'd bought a few more.

THE ROSE AT THE BACK OF THE HOUSE DECIDED TO STUDY EXPERIENCE SCIENTIFICALLY.

The rose at the back of the house talked like a rose, meaning that its voice was airborne and scented like a rose and that it could whisper easily, and sing easily, but never clog its own vocal chords with too much contradiction, or shout, or worry too hard. There was the passing of time. And the rose waited. Everything felt like it existed, or should exist, outdoors. Being inside, in a home, in a mansion, tucked in by a furnace, was simply bad health sense. Since Lord Burlington had planted the rose in memory of Samantha his lost love (who had consequently loved horsetomatoes and horsesauce so much, she had ended up poisoning herself. She hadn't known that poison could be nourishing if only taken in small amounts, and that too much of any of the same kind of nourishment would be poison. And she didn't know about taking the occasional purgatives either. Old fool, thought Lord Burlington, as he dug a circle in the dirt for the seed of the rose). He placed his tin can on the ground. The wind was blowing. The rose had been consuming sunlight for months now, had been watered with only the thermal waters of Swabia, had swayed under its glass jar, had felt protected without being in captivity, and therefore it was thriving and in peak bloom. It attracted all sorts of beneficial things. Green bugs and blue ones. It swung its neck down, traced the shape of a black box, and offered the bees its nodal secrets. Green butterflies and frosty blue ones. And everything is spiraling in the garden. This is a good omen. A spiral is the best geometrical shape or pattern to indicate that everything is alive in the garden to the degree that it should be alive. After all, the universe is shaped like a spiral! Dipping down around the rose at the back of the house. And everything is the shape of a helix. The plumeria. The quality of the herbs. You've never seen a better orange or pomegranate tree. Now the rose at the back of the house was very tall. It could almost reach to the roof of the cottage where Mr. Jones was spending his summer. Mr. Jones had been craving melon all year. Lord Burlington, fascinated with death, and having recently developed an interest in the new forms of the occult, tried to wheedle out of Jones everything he knew about the afterlife. What he really wanted to know, of course, but would not ask directly, was if death was final, and by that he meant an end to the war with the self, and if Mr. Jones had seen Samantha in her afterlife state, and if Jones had any messages or conversations with her to relay. Did she look as she always had, was she the same weight and heft, or was she stuck inside peculiar environments: glass boxes, image boxes, gold boxes, or nothing but knolls of barleygrass. (She had always been great at billiards and dinner conversation. In secret, Lord Burlington had commissioned an artist to make her a coarse, horse-hair billiards table. But now that she was gone, Lord Burlington couldn't bear to have the project come to fruition. And so the billiards table sat and rotted, half made, about ten feet from the fish pond. But Mr. Jones had reassured Lord Burlington that perhaps the object, although half made, was actually complete unto itself.) Everything has its own intentions for its life, said Jones. Maybe a whole horsehair billiards table did not want to come into existence. Or maybe, by coming into existence, the stars and the firmament would have been tossed from their orbits. One never knows these things, said Jones. Lord Burlington did not know what to make of Mr. Jones. In fact, the pair were like poisons and purgatives, sidling around each other, suspicious, easily jealous, competitive, but still wanting connection. You know, Burlington, Mr. Jones said one day, I've been to the mountains of Swabia. They are covered in the most beautiful orchids. Spider orchids, horse orchids, tiger orchids. Of every color you can imagine and then some: peach and orange and custard and reddish-pink, purplish black. Some have petals that are clear—entirely transparent—really mystical. And I have returned from the mountain, and I have seen the vistas, and I can say now, there is no such thing as Swabia. You don't know how to live. You don't know how to live without her. But we all have a predestined end. The bodily circuits of a child who lives only an hour will run their circuits just as the body of a centenarian. I have been to the mountains of Swabia, and I have climbed to the top, and I can say with certainty that there is no such thing as Swabia, and no orchid there can parallel the beauty of your Samantha. Lord Burlington had never felt so close to Jones. He nodded his head reticently, cast his eyes down on the rose, and thought himself an excellent gardener.

NOURISHMENT ATTEMPTED TO SCIENTIFICALLY STUDY THE SEED.

First and foremost, I wish to tell you that by your coming here tonight you are agreeing to spin on your heels and reel a little too. You have to put that in paragraph form. You have to be a guest at the party. You have to talk a little too loud and go home crying to whomever will listen. But Lord Burlington will have forgotten all about you by that time, I'm afraid. It was after the great war, and there had been ships departing from Swabian ports-of-call from time immemorial. But I thought you'd have brought that interesting book along with you, Esmeralda sighs. I was hoping we could read it together. Esmeralda is a sister, no, she is not a sister, she is someone's daughter, Mr. Jones's daughter, a hurricane, and she has the same eyes as all the fish in the pond. In the fish pond. No, by that I mean the sea. The weather. I was listening to you. You were wearing an orchid with a complicated name behind your ear and you'd said that you'd had enough to eat and didn't want to eat anymore. The world was changing. No, you said you were dancing. There was smoke in the sky. I love the way that orchid looks behind your ear. There is dancing. And the poisons come from the heavens in a kind of swirling motion or pattern, a spiral, if you will. It is because I am feeling very important today that I proudly don the official colors of Swabia. In the past, the Swabian army, and the Swabian navy, too, all the armed forces of Swabia, in fact, have honored me in this way, and I am proud and honored to be here. You are boring me today, and I don't know why, sighs Esmeralda. I used to read to you. You used to read to me. We used to take long walks and look at the fish in the fish pond, at the ducks in the sky, at the tiger orchids that grow wild on the grassy meadow. But now you tell too many lies. You take too much for granted and tomorrow is so scary, just the thought of tomorrow, that sometimes I can't even breathe. I don't know your name anymore, and to think that at one time we were neighbors. To think that we used to sail on ships. And when the Swabian coast was beautifully lit up, we could live for millions and millions of years, just like that, on gooseberry. Gooseberry coats, the good multi-colored ones, that is, and the way they looked. It was very easy to make a meal of the way we looked, then, when we were very beautiful and Swabia was still in its infancy. Ahem! *Dr. Honorable at your service.* Dr. Honorable is holding a medical instrument in his hand. It has been a very long day, and, elsewhere, Izetta is holding a candle and the fish in the fish pond are well and otherwise all is right with the world. But you have kept me waiting for far too long, Izetta sighs.

THE NEW APPROACH TO NATURE SOUGHT OUT TO STUDY A SUBMISSIVE DEPENDENCE ON OLD IDEAS SCIENTIFICALLY.

They knew that they were talented at inducing a crisis. Thus, they tucked themselves into blazes of scattershot, explosions in the atmosphere, brush fires, coups, exploitation, collapse, fistfights, rhetoric, ill-will, torn flags, and poisons. They approached Esmeralda, who was a hurricane, while she was sunning herself on the beach. She had on a new bathing suit she felt very good about and had marcelled her hair like a silent movie star. The colors of Swabia had always suited her complexion well, its mournful and refined palate of rooftops and commerce and dark flags, its green hills. And so she was red-cheeked and glistening under the sun. She saw the old ideas approaching, trying to look like everyman, like any man, like your average politician, your average struggling worker on the corner, your normal day of weather, your everyday item at the drugstore (shoe polish, for instance, or white shoelaces, or aspirin), an unremarkable cloud, a lost dime dropped in the sand. Stay away ten feet away from me, said Esmeralda to the old ideas, and she continued to address them, I'm sick and tired of having to reject things, denounce things, overhaul things. But the old ideas moved closer, even attempted humble and barely audible singing. *Now five years later on you've got the world at your feet. Success has been so easy for you. But don't forget it's me who put you where you are now. And I can put you back there too. Don't. Don't you want me? You know I can't believe it when I hear that you won't see me. Don't...* Esmeralda was feeling strong, a host to wide lungs, a gust of wind, and unforgiving, and confident, and she raised her hand at once. She dug her bare feet into the cool grains of sand. She said to old ideas, I'm sick of having to take sides, you see. I'm sick of saying, *your views about the universe are all wrong.* Still, in this world one must take a stand. And I'm siding with a new approach to nature. I realize that I can do this because I am one of those heavenly bodies that can actually be self-sufficient. I'm blessed with the ability of never needing to eat or take or consume anything again. My life, my heart, my thoughts, are self-generating, generous, and self-contained. I take nothing from you, nor from anyone, nor from the stars themselves. I have lots of friends in my life. I might be a hurricane, and cold and quick, purifying the smoke and chemicals in the sky, putting some things to bed and waking other things up, and I may only move in a kind of swirling motion or pattern, a spiral, but I know more than you ever will. The purpose of a hurricane is to expose. Realizing that it could not induce a crisis on the sandy shores of Swabia, and, in particular, a crisis in the form of a hurricane, the old ideas tucked a purple spider orchid behind one of Esmeralda's ears, but she would not be fooled. She threw the orchid into the ocean and started up her winds.

THE MOTION OF THE PLANETS SOUGHT OUT TO STUDY WHAT COULD NOT BE UNDERSTOOD SCIENTIFICALLY.

And that is scary. Mr. Jones was calling out the numbers of the people waiting in line. That's scary I tell you. There is too much clear-cutting going on. There is too much secret stuff going on in the Swabian forests in general, and it's like we are walking in circles around Lord Burlington's poolhouse, and the poolhouse is enormous, and it makes me want to cry, or it makes me just want to give up. Why, it makes me want to spend a small fortune on new clothes. But I was just a child. The heavens sent us to find out how fast we could run, but all we found out was that we had to wait. There was no movement, and all along I thought this was about movement. It was about fish. But I stand corrected. You stand corrected, this was not about fish. This has *never* been about fish. The people wait in line, and Jones, Mr. Jones, that is, is calling out their names. Their names and numbers are, however, the same. It is, in fact, just like Esmeralda once said. And all the fish in the fish pond. No, I am putting poison in my hair right now and there is not one of you that looks the same from one day to the next. You are wearing a different outfit every single day. And a very fashionable new look, I might add. I was looking at myself in the mirror. I was wearing nice new clothes. And suddenly I was ready to cry. I was ready to give up. What we wear is really poison. I always looked forward to trying on my new clothes, showing them to my best friend. The Swabian mountains were beautiful, especially if one looked at them from the window in Mr. Jones's living room. There is nothing new to say. It is dead quiet. Swabia is not real. We have a problem here. You are crying and thinking of giving up too frequently now. It is clear that you don't know how to live. You have lived before, though. You were visible then, in life, that is. Once upon a time, Jones, you were handsome and fashionable and a well-known figure. We used to see you and your mean gait all the time. We used to see you cutting a fine form on the dancefloor at the club. And the fish sigh. But fish don't sigh. But, man, that coat was nice. It was crystal clear and clean. And if you could have seen it at night from an upstairs window, and at just the right angle, man, loud! And looking expensive! It was good buying new clothes. It cheered us up on dark and gloomy days. It was good buying what one needed to buy. It made us feel healthy and alive and free. However, there is always going to be too much of this and too much of that and the color of the country is plum orchid, is gooseberry, and, Mr. Jones, is an old fool. This is Swabia, of course. I am lonely when I look around the room and don't see you sitting next to me. Well, then, tell the doctor, Jones says. As a matter of fact, that's exactly what I have been paying the doctor to look at! But I get lonely too, whispers Jones, and I've got a bone to pick with you. Look, listen, please let me whisper something in your ear just this one time. Let us restore the old intimacy, if even for a second. I could have cried; I felt like giving up. Given up or cried, and I didn't care which.

TREMENDOUS POTENTIAL SOUGHT OUT TO STUDY CHARITABLE MOTIVES SCIENTIFICALLY.

That's what the acting mayor was for. Tom Terrific. The Acting Mayor of All Swabia. He was there to fill in our gaps. He knew all about war, and he knew all about water. He had the best teeth in the city, the sturdiest, and the mossiest, he protected his people well, and his jawbone projected the best shadow anyone had ever seen. Mr. Jones has a theory about this. He claims that it's because of Tom Terrific's grin that he's now acting mayor, that, and because of his generally tidy and pleasing appearance, and his spaghetti-legged but authoritative gait, and I have never argued. But that is because I don't care much for wagering any guesses about politicians—who they are, why they are, where they are, how they got there, whether they are real or unreal, what they might want, and who put them in positions of power and influence in the first place. I don't trust anything I think or any information I get aside from what my gut tells me is true. But this time I was faced with the necessity of forming an opinion, of taking a side and deciding what the truth was. This is often what happens whenever you get into a discussion with Mr. Jones. He provokes thought, you see. It is because he is a real person. A great cook. He wears an apron and he has an iron pan and a whole cabinet full of flour and chilies of various degrees of potency. And real people tend to do that, to provoke thought. I needed to make some decisions. I needed to decide what I thought about this world of mine, of ours. I needed to decide what was real and what wasn't, what was good and what wasn't, what was worth making better and what was worth destroying, etc. When the sun came in my room that morning, soaking the curtains, arching over the knobs of my chest-of-drawers, I saw tremendous potential. It looked like a blaze of fire, or a glaze of it, or a black hat, or a partially eaten plum with the pit jutting out, depending on your point of view. Tremendous potential was at my back again. It was telling me not to be such a cad, a lazy shadow, a carousing, sleepy nymph, tucked into my sheets all day. Time to see the sky! it said. Time to see the clouds competing with the sun, time to see the shade on the ground, a gust of air. I rubbed my eyes and put on pants. Tremendous potential encouraged me to read the daily news. And that is when I discovered, as a citizen of Swabia, the story. The acting mayor was corrupt, you see. Corrupt again. And then again and again. He had all sorts of problems with lobbyists and other politicians who were also corrupt, and problems with the system, which was very corrupt, and he had the problem of never being able to tell the truth to anyone, especially to himself. This was because he spent so much money on his own pet projects, and had hired so many architects and physicians and general industrialists and general consultants and CEOs and astronomers. All this to get a new flag made for our town hall. To replace the black Swabian flag with a blue one, since black was now associated with anarchism. It had cost too much and now the town simply had no more money. And all due to the fact that the mayor was acting on whims of predestination. He was claiming that human time and human rhythms were no different than those of the very heavens themselves… the rings of Saturn, for example, the circuits of the spleen. He thought our politics to be just as organic and efficient as all general types of organization that you would find in nature. Most of his fellow general industrialists, corrupt lobbyists, and lying politicians agreed. And this, over a dinner table, while eating clams and lime-crusted steak. You should have seen the amount of clam shells in all the dumpsters behind the nice restaurants where they ate. However, they debated, argued, opposed, climaxed, and conjuncted before reaching an agreement about how big the flag should be and where it should be placed. Now that the town had no money, a lot had to change. For example, the orphanage had to shut down. And Swabia Elementary School had to increase class size. This sent me into a kind of foolish tizzy. I wanted to climb a tree and refuse to come out of the forest. All I could talk about now was getting myself a good pair of steel boots and getting back to the land. Foraging and lighting fires. Riding the backs of deer, swimming with grizzly bears. Sidling easily over power lines, eating all the edible weeds and seafoam I could find. I would stay in the forest and wait, until such a time that our city walls and city gates were gone, and when any hope at all could be placed inside our every-worrying minds and homes.

THE BODILY PLANETS sought out to study THE METHODOLOGY OF TIME scientifically.

Violence grows in the spleen but not in the heart. The heart grows in the head and then moves to Saturn and then on to the middle of the galaxy where it encounters either the morning or a nest of bluebirds. And the bluebirds are very happy in their home. And the sky is better than orange when you are waiting for the bus and there is just enough time to do all and anything you need to do. But this domestic stuff, this talk about home and hearth, this war, is getting boring. I thought you were going to talk about the garden. I thought you were going to talk about the fish pond and my horoscope and my fashionable new bathing suit. But very few of the little blue flags that flutter in the Swabian sky can actually be seen from Mr. Jones's living room window, yet one still enjoys just what one is not supposed to enjoy, and this is now, and it is not the present-time. Still, Samantha is coming over today and we are going to learn about diamond-backed rattlesnakes and all the other things that only Samantha knows about. She is very smart, you see, and unique and special, and has only been alive for about an hour or so with only about an hour or so to live. *Dr. Honorable here, at your service.* What do you mean? No one called a doctor? Mr. Jones is worried about his seeming lack of good fortune. He has spent too much time hoping for the best already today, and it is not yet tomorrow. Swabia is in a state of crisis. The world is set to turn on its axis and the planets, well, you know all about the planets. Lord Burlington met Samantha on a yacht, or rather, at a yacht party one memorable day in Swabia. But Samantha has only been alive for a minute or so and will only be alive for a few more minutes, yet she has already done so much, as much as anyone else, as much as anyone who has lived as long she has, that is. It's incredible. There is something to all of this. The description of a tree. It was Jones's fault. He was sitting on a patch of grass. He was sitting on a grassy meadow. I tell you that I have to go on belief and faith and trust from now on. I won't survive otherwise. Swabia won't survive. Did someone call a doctor? Dr. Honorable asks. Dr. Honorable has arrived on the scene, in the room, to be specific, in a puff, or rather, in a cloud of smoke. Who called a doctor? It is Samantha this time—and Samantha has only been on the scene for a minute or two and will only be on the scene for a minute or two more. Doctor, I have come here in advance of myself, I fear, Samantha says. I have come here before I am good and ready, and certainly before I am needed. It is always like that, friend, Dr. Honorable says. Then he gives his knee a great big slap and waits for the expected therapeutic outcome. It is the waiting that is good today, he thinks. It is the waiting, and the waiting only, that does, in fact, do a body good..

CRISIS SOUGHT OUT TO STUDY THE BLUE OX SCIENTIFICALLY.

The Blue Ox and her children were incredibly refined. The Blue Ox had a swaying, snaking diamond collar around her neck, and she always dabbed her neck with Gardenia Water, a very particular plant that had a very particular Swabian legend attached to it, related to the Swabian Coat of Arms. The Swabian nationalists liked to teach this legend to their children and sailors. They said that on the hill where the tiger orchids and the spider orchids grew, was one single clear, colorless flower reaching up out of a split in a yellow stone wall. A lone shepherdess (supposedly, a great-great-great grandmother of Lord Burlington, although he would deny having salt-of-the-earth roots) heard an uncontrollable, mystical, vegetative weeping across the hillside. But when the woman approached, all that she saw was a lone little transparent flower tossing its face against an overbearing wind, and the sound of a curtain knocking against a window. That was an apt description. And the plant began to speak. This the shepherdess swore. This is what she said she heard: I am so glad you are here. I could hear the world knocking outside my window, but it was always only about an hour away. Always only about an hour. The world was always ahead of itself, and not fully formed yet, and soon to vanish as well. And it was always knocking. That was the way of time. But I could never arrive to meet it where it was. The woman, being poor, didn't have much time. But our whole conversation depends upon the weather, said the plant. If it shifts even just a little bit, for example, if just one cloud becomes sour instead of bitter, colder instead of warmer, I will wither. The woman startled at that remark, and told the flower to hurry on up then with its proposal. And so it told her, beginning to trace the shape of a spiral with its head, I want humanity to divide itself into four groups, according to 1. Health, 2. Personality, 3. Taste, and 4. Income. The shepherd woman said, I will do my best, but that outcome will depend on the results of the Great Wars, the outcomes of games, and what will still remain after they are all over and done. The weather turned, the Gardenia Water faded, and in its place, so says the legend, was the Swabian Coat of Arms: a symbol split into four sections each with their own section and type of humanity. For example, teeming humanity, funny humanity, righteous humanity, cult humanity, enslaved humanity, pacifist humanity, lead-pipe humanity, and thought-wielding humanity, trickle-down humanity, sword-wielding humanity, idolatrous humanity, vicious humanity, nature-fearing mother-hating humanity, agrarian humanity, flavorless humanity, insulated humanity, crankshaft humanity, transgressive humanity, captivating humanity, sexually free humanity, compassionate humanity, typhoid humanity, patriarchal humanity, table-setting humanity, rhetorical humanity, cherry tree humanity, idealistic humanity, greedy humanity, futuristic humanity, building-block humanity, supremacist humanity, repressed humanity, sold-out humanity, courageous humanity, charitable humanity...

THE CRISIS SOUGHT OUT TO STUDY HUMAN RHYTHMS SCIENTIFICALLY.

The face is large, is very large, he said. And it is far worse than you could ever imagine. He would stop himself from time to time. He would stop his thinking. He would light fig cigarette after fig cigarette, turn the TV on and off. He would hold her hand. You are stopping yourself for no reason, you know, Tom. He said it rhythmically, and each step—it was called a beat—hurt his heart. Now, you know yourself. Now, you know yourself. And you are shouting and thinking about giving up. Tom Terrific was the man for the job. Everyone knew it by the way he stepped into the room, his gait. There was a gazebo on fire. There was a beautiful Blue Ox on a grassy meadow. You are the spitting image of a beautiful Blue Ox and you can't be stopped and the whole world is impressed by you and your good works! But, mister.... Tom's voice trailed off into the blue fig cigarette smoke that whirled in the air in front of him. I am so glad you are here. I am so glad you are never frightened. And all of this, of course, depends upon the weather, depends upon the outcome of the war. And, in one example, all Swabia will be saved and there will be no more screaming and no more clear-cutting the forest to make temporary and ugly and uncomfortable lodgings for the millions and millions of refugees that the war, that all the wars up to this point, have created. But it's that melodious and very pretty voice again, and idealism. Tom Terrific can do the job. He ashes his fig cigarette and surveys the Swabian coast. A genuine replica Swabian coat of arms, a very old one, glistened in the sun. Swabia was particularly beautiful on that occasion. You are smoking more fig cigarettes than you should, Tom. You will kill yourself. You will find yourself in an early grave, if you don't cut that bad behavior out. How many fig cigarettes do you smoke a day anyway? But culture depends, had depended for, seemingly, millions and millions of years, on the way of the world, on what was put into the world in the first place. The psychology was different this time, however. Tom Terrific was counting out change. The newspaper boy was waiting. An old song could be heard all up and down the Swabian coast. The song stuck, though, became a hit. There was a story to tell. You are running out of room here, mister. Swabia is getting too full to be comfortable, to be conducive to human life. And Tom sat in a chair in his Mayor of All Swabia office. He could hear the world outside his window. He often thought about beautiful things. Tom Terrific's hands, for instance, were beautiful. And how he loved his hands! The windows are wonderful in here, thought Tom, but the curtains are so damned tacky. Why doesn't someone open and close them, air them out, a little more often? Perhaps I would feel better about things if the windows were aired out once in a while. I think you mean the curtains, old man. You mean the solution to the problem is one of flexibility, says Tom Terrific. After all, diseases are inflatable, and I make a mistake when I emphasize the curtains. If only you would open your eyes, you would see that the world is already a better place. The Swabian coast sat prettily just outside the window. And there has to be depression, suffering, you know. It's inevitable. There has to be something. One can't just go on living in limbo forever.

CAUSE FOR CONCERN SOUGHT OUT TO STUDY FIG CIGARETTES SCIENTIFICALLY.

Esmeralda was up again late into the night, breathing against an open window, looking at the black sky and the blue stars. It was that Tom. He was always so relaxed. So like a tortoise. A folding chair. The opposite of a glass window or tacky curtains. He seemed so terrific on the surface, always lounging under that big oak tree, eating a damn peach, laughing. He was attractive because of his good health. His skin was gilded with the thermal waters of Swabia. No one seemed as healthy as Tom Terrific. No one's muscles seemed as healthy as Tom's. No one's gait was as casual and entitled. He was all teeth. But he had that terrible habit, always rolling and stuffing fig cigarettes, playing the magic trick where he would roll them in-between each finger faster than the eye could detect. Was that the habit, or addiction, that would get him in the end? When Esmeralda walked beneath the tree in the grassy meadow, he would always call out to her. His voice seemed true enough, full of relaxed substance and principle, and neither one in excess. He said, I can see the whole sweep of the land from here in its entirety. The whole Swabian coast. Let me take you out some time. To the movies, or to a restaurant. One with candles and bad electricity. And homemade red sauce and horsesauce. It will be more than pleasant. He stood as if he held many meadows in his fist. She noticed that he was looking out over the vista, down on all the little blue Swabian flags jutting out of the tile rooftops. Each one rippling the same way, like the tails of fish doggedly parting water. She felt the wind rising from the cliffs. And there was salt in the air. He always looked out and over versus *at* something. She would say to him, no one can see anything in its entirety. And she would continue to walk wherever it was that she was heading. But one day Tom Terrific wore her down. Perhaps it was his great health. Or the goddamned peach. Or perhaps it was election year rhetoric—everyone's thoughts were skewed back and forth between charitable motives and skepticism. Do you really want to take me out? she said. Do you even know how much things cost these days? Tom Terrific, biting into an apple replied, well, you still see me laughing. That's what rebellion is all about. Esmeralda bought herself a new green dress, forest green, cut to flatter, and made to make her look beautiful, and at dinner she tried to order the most appropriate item on the menu. The menu was categorized according to humour and type: salty, bitter, sour, and sweet. Vegetable, fish, fowl, and others. She ordered a glass of gooseberry wine and an acorn salad with spinach and horsedressing. She talked about the frightening patterns in the weather. But Tom Terrific was staring out the window, parting the curtains in the restaurant. Such nice curtains. Red and gauzy and still. Well-sewn and tidy. Such good taste. I will go back to the tree and smoke a fig cigarette. I will go back there and die a slow death. And your views on the universe are all wrong. He did not realize that he had said the last two statements out loud. Esmeralda had more than cause for concern. She handed him a small piece of paper. She had gone through this once before with a friend. Call this clinician, she admonished, for he is quite Honorable. I think, in my esteem. She was very disappointed. Tom Terrific had started to look handsome over dinner, had started to sound not dissimilar to an odd-lot intellectual, or an eccentric manifesto, and she was a hard one to please. Secretly, before they parted ways, she stole a fig cigarette from out of his shirt pocket and put it in her purse. For later, she thought, knowing that when the spirit suffers, so does the body. They call the reverse process the *ense spirituale*, or cause for concern. The body influencing the spirit right back.

THE FOUR HUMOURS SOUGHT OUT TO STUDY THE CAUSE SCIENTIFICALLY.

An ordinary Swabian citizen's first mistake is trying to decide how much things cost. After all, a half-eaten and thoughtlessly discarded lunch can be more expensive than a fig cigarette, if one really wants it to be. But that logic would make an ordinary Swabian citizen cringe. And one should never give the impression of living too large off the land, especially if you are looking to impress the fact upon ordinary Swabian citizens, that is, Lord Burlington sneers. In fact, a problem occurs every time an ordinary Swabian citizen raises his or her hand. And there is a danger, in the end, of the self, being lost, if that makes sense? Lord Burlington puts down his pointer, and stands, hands on hips. The lecture is over, but there is a beautiful Blue Ox on a grassy meadow. And I just can't remember the names of all the different types of orchids. There are so many of them and they are all so varied and sometimes I wish I were dead. Well, Jones, says Lord Burlington, laughing, if you'd just stop looking in the mirror, you probably would have noticed by now. There is a good sized audience for Lord Burlington's Lecture Series that night. They have come to watch the singing and dancing, the carousing, and fire. I can't be seen from the top of the hill, thinks Mr. Jones. I will go there and die a slow death. I am so humiliated. Well, Jones, says Lord Burlington, laughing, if you'd just stop looking in the mirror, you probably would have noticed by now. Mr. Jones reaches the top of the hill. He is laughing at his own good health. He is in quite good health, despite his age. And, funny, because Tom Terrific smokes too many fig cigarettes and can climb the hill and take his seat just fine. And, funny, because Tom Terrific has smoked a fig cigarette every single day since he was nine years old and still can do the meanest jig of all when there is dancing under the gazebo after Lord Burlington's Lecture Series. In fact, Tom Terrific is terrific because of how many fig cigarettes he consumes in a day and because of how much he chokes and coughs and the ways in which he loves Esmeralda in spite of it all. It is heady stuff at Lord Burlington's Lecture Series that night. And it is sad stuff as well. Mr. Jones is puffing his chest in and out. He is making a muscle, flexing his arms. He is sticking his head right out of the dirt that day, just like any ordinary Swabian citizen would. At least, that's what Mr. Jones thinks until he sees a beautiful Blue Ox off on the horizon.

> *The Blue Ox is giant, sir. I saw it over by the well.*
> *The Blue Ox is enormous, sir, but I swear it is sad.*
> *Why, yesterday, and it was only yesterday,*
> *because today is just today.*
> *Why, it was only yesterday that I saw a big Blue Ox*
> *and it was crying.*

And you call that election year rhetoric, Jones? Well, says Lord Burlington, laughing, if you'd just stop looking in the mirror, you probably would have noticed by now. There is smoke from millions and millions of fig cigarettes in the air, and there are too many tall trees on the ground. Clear-cutting. Everyone has grown melancholy because of the rain. The wind blows. There is a grassy meadow and cows and geese. A beautiful Blue Ox. Esmeralda looks on the ground and is pleasantly surprised not to see the grave of her father, Mr. Jones. It is early fall and the ground is covered with acorns. There will be plenty of acorns this year, Esmeralda sighs. She has already started the catalog in her mind: acorn candy, acorn bread, acorn soup, acorn salad with spinach and horsesauce dressing...

THE SPIRIT sought out to study MANKIND'S WICKEDNESS scientifically.

Forget about it, man. Forget about it, man, said Cecil, lounging by the pool, putting a toothpick through a green olive. Forget about it so that you can build things. Just then the sky started to rain and the smell of gooseberries and the overpowering odor of work gloves filled the air. And even by the pool. And even here there was death all around, but the people sitting poolside thought they were very healthy. After all, Lord Burlington was now in charge, and opened his gates up to the public once a week so that they could enjoy the warm weather. There was a whole collection of wildlife that he would place on the lawn as well, just for the kids. White rabbits and red squirrels, shameless wolverines, gentlemanly penguins, noncommittal salamanders, skittish pheasants, and forlorn kestrels. Samantha was in the garden with a clipboard in one hand, trying to classify all the animals and plants on the Burlington estate. She had split a piece of paper into two columns. One side was for things that were utopian and the other for things that were not.

Utopian	Not Utopian
the rose at the back of the house	forlorn kestrels
sorrel	horsetomatoes
barleygrass	shameless wolverines
the cherry tree	the red fish
gentlemanly penguins	bitter gourd

But the kids today, they are jaded, narcissistic. Forget about it, man, Cecil said again. Well, said Lord Burlington, laughing. He straightened his vest

and his burgundy waistcoat and raised his wineglass full of red horsetomato wine. Cecil snapped the elastic band of his velvet swimming trunks. It
was all very classy. Here is the thing, Cecil said, the kids today. They are the
way they are because of the war. And we are the way we are because of the
war, and because of election year rhetoric. He thought that he was speaking something true, but he was pushing another little olive around in his
crystal glass, causing it to go in a loop, like a bull trapped in a rodeo ring,
or a rope knotted in a figure-eight. Everything is the way it is on account
of the war. And the bodies in the pool were real. Remember when Swabia
was oceanic? I said, and I truly remembered when the nation was set right.
So concrete. Now people are happy, but people can be happy when death
is all around. They can have their various coping mechanisms. Like, for
example, noticing all the beautiful colors of the earth and how it trembles
because of its colors. Or they float on inner tubes in the pool, staring at the
white rabbits chewing barleygrass and fig stems as if they were not real.
Nothing is real. Nothing is to be trusted, and your senses least of all. And
you are good and you are not good. And there is a stain and there isn't a
stain. And whether you're above ground or you're not is the real question.
Are there real questions? And this is because of the war. People are very
concerned. People are very concerned about the state of Swabia. People are
very concerned about the state of Dalmatia or Salmatia. It is morning on
Lord Burlington's estate. No, it is afternoon, and the sun is ballooning and
dripping, and leaves are dripping and falling, and moods are falling and
rising, and Lord Burlington is rising from his seat and greeting the public
(the common man?), and everyone's spirits are not swimming and are not
well. And this could have been an idyllic time, thinks Samantha. And I
must hold this knowledge in silence. It is a terrible weight.

THE MANIFESTATION SOUGHT OUT TO STUDY FIG CIGARETTES SCIENTIFICALLY.

Phooey, the army just cannot do that to a man, Jones, I don't care what you say. Mr. Jones has put too much weight on one foot. He has, perhaps, leaned a little awkwardly while standing. Lord Burlington, I just want to tell you... Well, says Lord Burlington, laughing, if you'd just stop looking in the mirror, Jones, you would probably have noticed by now. Ha ha. The earth trembles because of all of its colors. There is moss growing in the fish pond. I refuse to respond to you, Jones. You have become an annoyance. And I remember when Swabia was blue, and the good kind of blue, too. There is an alligator in a swamp. And Lord Burlington, well, Lord Burlington loves what he loves. There is a multi-colored and, incidentally, very fashionable gooseberry coat on the ground that used to belong to Lord Burlington's best friend Tom Terrific. However, one doesn't see a Tom Terrific, the likes of a Tom Terrific, around here anymore. It is morning in Swabia. Great cargo ships leave the Swabian coast. Millions and millions of cartons of fig cigarettes will leave Swabia via the sea on this day alone. And barrels of rice perfected in a lab. And flag paper for tiny blue Swabian flags, millions and millions of them. However, there is a disruption. A fever dream. Esmeralda is counting out acorns. The fish swim in lazy circles in the fish pond and this is during an idyllic time before there was fever or disease or anything else that anyone had to carry too far. The war is over. It has just been announced on the radio. Swabia is liberated. The likes of Lord Burlington. Now the likes of Lord Burlington and Tom Terrific and the whole upper class Swabian scene. The army, the navy. The crisis. This is because of the war. All things in Swabia are the way they are on account of the war. Even the horses. Even the colors of the oxen. The fish pond is teeming with fish. The Swabian coast is a great place from which to set sail. It is a great place to build things. I will make a painting, thinks Mr. Jones. Mr. Jones has walked millions and millions of miles in a single minute and he is not even tired. He is in tip-top shape. His gooseberry coat is the only thing slowing him down. And, man, that coat was nice. It was loud! When that coat walked into the room things happened. That coat. You'd put that coat on… And just forget about it, man. But Swabia is teeming. The goats, the turkeys, the chickens, the dinosaurs, the pterosaurs. The fish pond is the place where it all began and even if there is only standing water and death all around now, the people are happy. There is no more war. There is no place for depression or bad feelings or melancholy. *Why, it is Dr. Honorable at your service.* Dr. Honorable defies description. He is, in fact, the only one who knows. The only one who holds the knowledge of exactly how a gooseberry coat is put together. And he holds the knowledge all by himself. It is, in fact, a terrible weight, a lot to bear, but he is not going to tell anyone. In fact, he'll never breath a word of it to anyone, ever, because Dr. Honorable is, after all, an honorable man.

IZETTA SOUGHT OUT TO STUDY BALNEOLOGY SCIENTIFICALLY.

She was out in the alley again, with a bare, cream-colored slip on, opening the drawer. Inside was a ripe orange, a flashlight, garters, a shoehorn, and several pairs of men's brown socks. The sun cascaded off of her shoulders, then glided onto her elbows, and finally illuminated her manicured thumbnails. Inside the drawer was a picture of the Swabian coast. It was glossy and creased at the middle. In the photo, the sea was a lucky shade of blue. Above the sea were the stone houses, each with a little black flag and a crest on the front, which bore many symbols divided into four parts. If only Swabia were more than just an idea. She closed the drawer. She felt herself imperfect. And she hadn't cut the celery for the stew, and that was a necessary ingredient. There was still Jones to consider. And the fricassee. That was the starter. And the purple grapes. The stew was really for him and his friends. And Mr. Jones, despite being magnetic and wholly unable to be duplicated, still would be disappointed at the taste of a missing ingredient. Izetta drooped at the thought and tugged her hemline. She was the kind of—classifiable—person who really and truly did not like to hurt anyone else, and she spent most of her time thinking about how not to hurt people. She spent so much time thinking about how not to hurt people. How to care for, and how not to hurt people. How to make *better*, and not to make *worse*. The sun was turning red as it got darker in the alley. And somewhere there was water leaking and trickling down a cement wall. The spider in the alley was tracking it, and climbing upwards. And because Izetta cared, because Izetta did not want to hurt other people, because Izetta was not a coward, the thought of not putting celery in the stew fixated so strongly. And the hope of preventing the possibility of Mr. Jones's potential displeasure, even if slight. He is too polite when he is unhappy. It's the striped tie. It's the gooseberry coat slouched on the hat-stand by my front door. At their last dinner party Samantha had reamed Mr. Jones while pointing at him—And suffering and depression are *not* inevitable. You're problems are cherry-picked, Jones, *cherry-picked*! Often Izetta would bare her heart to the sun and to the other elements (the *water*, the *wind*, etc.) because she had nothing to hide. She abhorred crime. She hated circuses, especially the way they treated the elephants. And she would never think of hunting or fishing just for sport, never. She would never try to make money at a racetrack. There are problems everywhere we look, she thought, and once again she looked at the stellar blue Swabian ocean in the postcard, and the white sands, which would fall through your fingers with a slight texture. The sand was as smooth as a banana peel. A pocket of pollen. A gust of twine. A rock of leaves. The stew would have to be splendid. There was Jones to consider, after all. Izetta was the classifiable kind of person who would diffuse a hurricane before it ever arrived in her proximity. She wanted to make something better. She abhorred the image box. Its smell of shark fins. She was in the alley again, closing the drawer, and then opening the door to the dark little room with the antique lamp. She thought to herself, because she had been studying it scientifically, there are two ways people can hurt each other. Intentionally—by the unified force of thought, feeling and will. Or unintentionally. Invisibly. That is why so many people have sicknesses of the spirit and of the will. This will-power of mine is a creature of my spirit. And some day, some day I will hurt no one. She returned to her thoughts on balneology. If only there was such a place as Swabia. If only the healing waters were real, the steambaths scented with dog orchids and water gardenias, the pools of healing fish that ate the dead skin off of your hands, the underground springs that disappeared when the weather shifted. Then I could become an expert at making things better. Or at least marry one. A handsome balneologist with hair like a palomino. A Tom Terrific. A successful, kind man with his own gooseberry coat and well-polished shoes. Or kind woman. Or kind spider. She was in the alley opening up the drawer, taking out the picture of the Swabian coast. Luckily for her, the picture was taken right after the retreat and reformation of the Swabian navy. So the picture looked placid and the water was blindingly blue, unmoved, and continuously calm.

THE SPIRIT SOUGHT OUT TO STUDY HOME SCIENTIFICALLY.

Gazing in the fish pond and scientifically studying the many and various multi-colored fish was, for Izetta, tantamount to life itself, or rather, that which she lived for. Izetta had always abhorred crime, or anything else she couldn't quite get a bead on, but, still, it was, with her busy schedule, quite a lot to have to confront on a daily basis. The thing is, Jones, Lord Burlington says, during the stew, and after the lowering and folding of the tiny new blue Swabian flags has been completed for the day, you must find esteem within your own well, so to speak. You must find it by taking a hard look at each and every thing you hold dear. Let's take you for example, Jones. Inside of two weeks this crisis will be done. The war will be over. And you will be resting by yourself on your patch of grass all over again. Well, it is where I want to be, but I won't dwell on it, says Mr. Jones. And everyone is sitting, and there is a general lessening, or slowing, or something... A revised version of the Swabian national anthem has been recorded and is playing on every radio throughout the land. And soiled and dusty curtains, and candelabras, and mahogany, and fixed terraces. Why, the whole world is a better place when the forest is finally on fire, when it lets itself burn to the ground, or so it is thought. Still, there is a danger in nature and in gnashing one's teeth and in asking for honor and all that stuff, or so it is thought. I am Tom Terrific, and I am here to tell you that I can barely speak, and if I were a better man I might be able to hold my head above the water of this fish pond as well. It is worth pointing out. There are problems everywhere one looks. The recent reforms in the Swabian navy. Despite recent reforms in the Swabian navy. Tonight, Lord Burlington looks every one of his millions and millions of years. It is past seven o'clock, and Lord Burlington is not ready to go home. He has left his briefcase on the floor of the lecture hall where he has been spending so much of his time lately. He is going to go shopping for clothes very soon. He is going to buy the extremely fashionable multi-colored gooseberry coat that he has seen hanging in a store window. Izetta is in the alley, opening a dresser drawer. I have learned a lot about the subject of criminality, she thinks. She has no best friend. And who doesn't remember the name of their best friend from second grade? asks Tom Terrific. Why, my best friend from second grade was you, Burlington. This is obvious, of course, and there is still Jones to consider. There is a happy band of students from the Swabian Medical College who want to learn about him. They want to come over to his house and study him and take notes on everything he says and does. But Mr. Jones feels free, free for once, as he stares across the grassy meadow. He has written the students' professor, Dr. Honorable, a short but very polite message. He is simply not up for visitors that day. And Izetta is opening a dresser drawer in the alley. There is a solitary sock and a perfume smelling picture postcard of the famous blue Swabian coast inside the dresser drawer. Izetta puts on the sock, lifts the scented postcard to her nose and cries. And, to think, it is said that a gooseberry coat is not the most important thing after all, says Lord Burlington.

THE SPIRIT DECIDED TO STUDY GOODWILL SCIENTIFICALLY.

Hey, Honorable, says Esmeralda, hand me one of those Swabian squares, the fig ones in the purple packet. I don't know what you're talking about, says Dr. Honorable, laughing. He is trying to make himself look empty and useless. C'mon, Honorable, I know your secret vices, she says, You are my good and true ally, which is saying everything. And I'm not being unduly wistful, and there are no two ways of saying it. You see, I know when you're telling me filthy lies about the things that I know to be true. That is an all-important skill, says Honorable, tweaking his jacket pocket and producing none other than a slender little Swabian fig square. The white wrapping on the outside of the cigarette looks as delicate as flag paper. Everything looks flimsy and a little filmy. Everything is really good now. The war is over and Esmeralda has settled into a comfortable life. She has a nice apartment with a good couch, and on the weekends she goes out on dates with handsome professionals: balneologists, watchmakers, doctors, Lord _____, flag paper manufacturers, people who are the hub of the center of commerce. She has dinners with round orange beacons, elemental zests, loquacious volcanoes, well-coiffed sunsets, shy barometers, frank auroras, stingy tidal waves, tender mudslides. She has a nice wardrobe and can charge things to her credit card. And she is in love so much and so often that she is spending all her money. But Dr. Honorable, being her good and true ally, is secretly worried. He thinks he feels her pain as acutely as he feels his own. And the war is over but Jones is dead again, lost to the war effort, his body was real, and there was a pool of blood, and a knife, and a gun, and a mace, and a battleaxe, and a longsword, and a dagger, and a pistol, and a raygun, and a javelin, and a club, and a wrack, and an iron maiden, and a scimitar, and a poison, and another kind of poison, and sand in the lungs, and a blunt instrument, and a missing hand, and brass knuckles, and a club, and a bludgeon, and a truncheon, and a stick, and noxious vapors, and a slingshot, and a crossbow, and Esmeralda is refusing to discuss this. Her problems stem from the inside out. Because the war is over. Everything is really good now. Each citizen can define themselves on their own terms. And no one has done anyone any bodily harm in at least a week or two. And who could remember the last time that happened? Most of the time there are problems everywhere you look. And Dr. Honorable knows Esmeralda. He knows when she is healthy and when she is sick, and this makes him her true ally. Hey, Honorable, look out there, over the coast. Do you see that flock of seabirds? Should I send them a good gust of wind? Make it as cold as a cavern, as a gulch, so that they shiver and wake up out of their dreaming? Now, Dr. Honorable has been Esmeralda's best friend since the second grade, and he knows that it isn't like her to say such things, she is seeing the universe all wrong, and he knows therefore to be worried, and to therefore try and produce a curative effect upon her— either through language or through medicine or through science or through simple care (i.e. seeing outside himself). The four classifiable forms that a cure can take. When they go to sleep that night in their respective apartments, he will try many different things, all of them equally real. He will take a picture of Esmeralda and Mr. Jones that she ripped in two and glue it back together again. That will be medicine. And he will take a picture of her and paint a new mouth over her old one so that she is smiling. And that will help. And he will give her aspirin, that will be good, and sulphur, as well as talk therapy, that will also be medicine. And he will give her horsetomato soup and some wholesome dark bread. And then when they go to sleep, each in their respective homes, he will try to walk over to her dream house and knock on the door. She'll refuse but she'll open the latch to the chimney and he'll float down, landing feet first on the soft quiet carpet in his gooseberry shoes. He'll light a fire and light his mahogany pipe, fill it with fig tobacco. And they'll talk. Openly and honestly and figuratively. And his dream will be fulfilled through the medium of words and she will not consciously register this dream. But this dream will help her. And he'll take this knowledge secretly because he's a man. And that will be medicine. After all, if Esmeralda fell to dissipation, that would not only be bad for her, but for the whole of Swabia, as well as the air itself. And we can't risk more hurricanes. Or more birds being snapped out of their sleep by unseasonable weather and winds. Too many have already been lost that way, and we can't afford to lose yet another. Not even one. We cannot suffer one more loss. There are no two ways of saying it. We cannot suffer one more loss.

THE ARDENT ATTEMPTED TO SCIENTIFICALLY STUDY THE INFLAMED OPPONENT.

And your buddy old pal is here, Terrific. *Dr. Honorable at your service.* You are my ally, my good and true ally and friend. The Swabian coast is lit up tonight. There is no other way of saying it: Swabia is beautiful, even to an unrepentant sinner like me, laughs Lord Burlington. *Dr. Honorable at your service.* I was unduly wistful, adds Mr. Jones. There is a large and beautiful Blue Ox grazing on a grassy meadow. The forest is a beautiful place at night. There are elderberry trees and geese and flying lizards and living room furniture and a really gorgeous sperm whale. You should come here often. You should fly tiny blue Swabian flags from every tree and bush. But at night I am less able to see what I need to see, says Tom Terrific. *Dr. Honorable at your service.* But this time the problems seem to stem from the inside out, and, thus, no one can safely say what's wrong. Spirit fights spirit, and may the best spirit win. It has been at least a week or two since I did you bodily harm, says Lord Burlington. In fact, I have not done anyone bodily harm in at least a week or two. However, balneology is just another discipline, I'm afraid. Not magic. I'm sorry. A therapeutic spring up in the mountains, or, what I mean to say is that there are fish in the fish pond and Mr. Jones is dead and the war is over and everything is really cool now. Cecil, dude, hand me one of those Swabian squares. Cecil stares sadly at the ground. Now he too knows that Jones really is dead and that there truly is no one left to talk to. The cigarettes, you idiot. The fig ones in the purple packet. And I tell you I love you, whether I mean it or not, says Dr. Honorable. Expressions of love are what people need when their spirits are under attack. I would just feed them, give them what they want to eat. It's easier that way, says Samantha, putting away a deck of cards. There is no easier way of saying what I want to say. There is no other way to tell you that I love you. But the war is over. And it's a laugh, a real riot. Why, the apocalypse had barely begun before the truth was out of the bag. Lord Burlington, at last, sees the opening he's been waiting for all night. He closes his eyes and imagines his enemy as a dark spot against a light blue wall. He imagines all the pain his spirit will inflict and dances and sings and offers to charge everyone's dinner to his credit card. And it is useless, ultimately, to resist, thinks Lord Burlington with a smile. Indeed, Lord Burlington believes he feels everyone else's pain as acutely as he feels his own. He is wrong, of course, and I, Dr. Honorable, am here to explain to you just how wrong he is. I call this case, *Case Study #194*, or rather, *Koalas and Cabbage: A Match Made in Heaven?*

THE SUCCESSFUL CURE DECIDED TO STUDY OCCUPATIONAL DISEASES SCIENTIFICALLY.

And also the diseases of un-occupations: laziness, wealth, and lounging. As such, the Successful Cure, beaming and pulsating in the shape of a blue orb, a whole symbol, began to trod down the path leading to the estate belonging to the wealthiest man in all of Swabia, none other than Lord Burlington. Lord Burlington was wicking his forehead with a hand towel. That morning he had been most concerned about the blight that had suddenly hit his gooseberry bushes, and the rose at the back of the house. The rose had turned ashen purple and was drooping petals, one by one, onto the ground. And Samantha had one more time been born, arrived on the scene, and died before she was needed. Is there a doctor in the house? he shouted to the wind, to the high chainlink fence surrounding his tennis courts, and his badminton courts, and the wind carried his voice as far as the gate, and then the wind stopped. Cecil sees Lord Burlington drooped over his little flower, trying to nudge it softly with his hands. He thinks it is funny and sad at the same time, and he snaps the elastic band of his velvet swimming trunks. Do you remember Jones, man? he calls out to Burlington, tightly rolling a fig cigarette inside some flag paper. I feel like I have no one to talk to anymore. And at the mention of Mr. Jones, Lord Burlington gets angry. Jones should have known better than to make such a tactical misstep during wartime. For a minute he feels pain at the loss of Mr. Jones, his colleague, friend. A real pain, too, and not an imaginary one! He is feeling pain and not just observing life, but feeling it. And the feeling is *pain*, and invigoratingly sour. That's none of your fucking business how I feel about Jones, Cecil, Lord Burlington says, laughing. Mr. Jones is underground. A tactical error by the Swabian Navy. And now Jones can only lie in his grave and think. That's a pool of blood beside me, idiots. A pool of blood, you idiots. Don't you even know what blood looks like? And do you know how fucking shiteously boring a pool of blood is? And this is not an imaginary condition, thinks Jones. And Jones, thank fortune, unlike other men (because he is unlike other men) can't imagine what his enemies look like, and therefore cannot picture what he would to do to them. Whether he would hurt them, trick them, or try no strategies at all. Just be authentic. Be himself. Or offer them a warm coat, a fig cigarette. The enemy is not a cell gone wrong, or a heathen idiom, or a green pustule, or a fig cigarette, or this plant or that one, or this animal or that one, or an illness, or a weapon, or this or that amount of money, or a human in a starched uniform, clanking a metal cup against a gate, or a human in a uniform forcing himself or herself upon another, or upon a territory, or into someone's life where they don't belong, or a human in a uniform causing someone bodily harm. When Mr. Jones closes his eyes, when he seals his eyes shut against the dirt crumbling down onto his face and shirt, and seals them shut against the beautiful Swabian coast and the beautiful Swabian night and the beautiful Swabian skyline and the eagles circling above him and the all the blue Swabian flags snapping in unison in the harshest winds and all the dehydrated hills and gooseberry trees, he imagines no enemies. *The enemy is simply your path to freedom. The enemy is simply your friend in disguise. The enemy is simply a trigger for the pain you already have.* Mr. Jones closes his eyes, he imagines no enemies. And suddenly Jones is sitting on a hill watching the world fall to bits. Suddenly he is out of the grave, watching a sunset, bleak and vibrant at the same time, and it will let you ask it as many questions as you want to. And Jones knows that at this hour everyone is hard to hear. Everyone has a hard time hearing everyone else. Everyone has a hard time hearing and seeing everyone else. And suddenly the Blue Ox is trotting through the beautiful field, gnawing softly and sweetly on the barleygrasses and on dog orchids, which are scented like honey and limeaid. The Blue Ox is giant and beautiful and matches the sky. Greetings, Blue Ox, says Jones. It is a fine day, a fine dusk, she says, speaking in her refined voice that funnels down into your ears like a good glass of wine. It's good to listen to her with your ears, quite pleasant. And since when have you stopped living on Lord Burlington's estate? asks Jones. At the mention of Burlington's name, the Blue Ox is stunned. She chokes a little. She sharpens, sputters and drops her sweetgrass and her dog orchids and says, sounding less polite, none of your fucking business! I'm sorry, Jones says, I didn't realize there was a sore spot between you both. I got tired of his estate, she says again, looking off at the sunset, sinking below the gooseberry bushes and the gooseberry trees, and all the coastal flags. In the end, it was his spacious house. All the chinks in the walls, and the drafts blowing in. And if you listened with your ears, you heard that the estate was about to crumble, become a successor to time itself. Did you hear the gazebo was on fire? I would rather be alive and be healthy than be there. Jones listens to her with his ears and heart, and he nods. Has anyone put two and two together in this stinking place, he thinks? Maybe the Blue Ox has and maybe he himself hasn't. He decides it's time to get back to work. He gathers his books and his picnic basket. Time to resume my studies, he thinks. The world is so heavy these days. It tires one out so fast. I will have to wait for the caffeine to kick in. He trods down the lane, sees the city lights. He bears the same intention, the same intention as always. It never ends. To save all that he can.

THE WAXEN IMAGE ATTEMPTED TO SCIENTIFICALLY STUDY ITS OWN NATURE.

Forces his hand every time, or if you have lived as long as I have... And, at that, Lord Burlington closes his Book, and then closes his eyes, and then falls asleep with a tremendous smile of satisfaction stuck on his lips. You are dreaming of that which is not there. Your dreams are a last resort. You are sort of at home, but not at all at home. And when you listen very carefully, all sorts of tremendous opportunities arise. This pattern becomes me today, says Lord Burlington in his sleep, and it is as if—as if... as if... All of Swabia has answered a similarly patriotic call. In fact, all of Swabia will be surrendering today, and there is going to be a great celebration afterwards. Cecil is going in circles, trying to remember something important. It was not something he was supposed to tell Lord Burlington, rather, something about the room he was born in. I want a vacation day, says Dr. Honorable, there has been too much work around here lately, and I am getting very tired. Dr. Honorable gets in his car and drives up the Swabian coast. He is an avid bird watcher and his binoculars and gloves are in the back seat of the car. There is no population. Swabia is deserted. You have to make it home before the people come around, man. You totally have to dig your hole in the ground after everyone has gone. And, dude, that's totally what they forget to tell you, Cecil exclaims. He is concealing the sealing wax for his fig cigarettes in an envelope on the floor of the car. Dr. Honorable is a bit of dork, thinks Cecil, a bit slow on the uptake for a physician, but, still, he makes a pretty cool traveling companion. And Swabia, well, we know what Swabia can do! I want to sit under a tree, says Esmeralda. I want to sit under a tree and watch the gooseberry bushes grow. The gooseberry blossoms are gorgeous at this time of year. This is funny, thinks Jones, a funny predicament to find oneself in. Funny and sad at the same time. The way no one has put two and two together. I am underground. Get it? I am literally underground. And I have a weight here and a weight there and it does really, honestly hurt most of the time to be me, and it is actually not imaginary pain at all. Oh no! exclaims Dr. Honorable. What? Did you say something, man? asks Cecil, opening his eyes. They are calling me *again*. I'll never get any of my vacation time now. I can drop you off here, pick you up later, if you want, young man, Dr. Honorable says to Cecil. But I was just sitting here minding my own business, not thinking of you at all, father, sighs Esmeralda. But I need you! screams Mr. Jones. I need you. Esmeralda has to get up now. She has to take her gooseberry coat and her book and her picnic basket and head back home. Suddenly, the sky has grown cloudy. Suddenly, it has become very cold. Suddenly, we are sitting on a high hill and watching the world get torn to bits all over again. But you loved once, old man. I know you did. You loved and lost. You can't deny it. And, at that, Lord Burlington laughs and laughs, for he knows now that it was he himself who caused the headache that's been killing him for weeks.

THE FIRST FOUR BOOKS SOUGHT OUT TO STUDY THE HEATHEN IDIOM SCIENTIFICALLY.

It is raining, Burlington, I swear it is. You can hear the water on the roof. It was raining. Rain all up and down the Swabian coast, and millions and millions of thoughts of the heathen idiom lodged inside their brains that evening. The way they sat together in Lord Burlington's smoke-filled poolhouse, gloomily, lost amid their studies. And by now you ought to know the first four books by heart, says Lord Burlington. Why, it's just a rehash of what every ordinary Swabian citizen already knows anyway. For example, look at Jones here! Jones, gentlemen, is always looking for answers, forever trying to find that special secret way to keep his hopes and dreams intact, yet all he ever comes up with is the heathen idiom! And infinite versions of it, to boot! Not that that's a bad thing, in and of itself... Mr. Jones is stunned at the sudden scrutiny, at the sudden change in atmosphere at Lord Burlington's poolhouse. He has come there that evening for a little collegiality, for what he believed would be a modest and friendly scholarly supplement to Lord Burlington's most recent lecture. But because you love to smoke fig cigarettes in the morning, sir, you will die. Tom Terrific does not believe a word anyone says about Swabian fig cigarettes. *I was working as a waitress in a cocktail bar...* And if only the world were a better place, and if only things were a little less odd. If only you were a little less odd, Jones, sneers Lord Burlington. Leaving so soon? This lack of communication, thinks Jones, will be the death of me. I swear it was better here before the war, before all those odd-lot intellectuals and young international architects came, and, actually, before all the death and destruction. *Dr. Honorable at your service.* Maybe I should just give up, thinks Mr. Jones.

At the very least, someone might have told me how warm it was going to be underground. I would have dressed more appropriately! In a far off place, Izetta is rummaging around in the closet. She is happy when she sees something she likes. The garment she selects to wear that day is very warm and brown and red and green and yellow and made of gooseberry, and the good kind of gooseberry, too, not the synthetic kind that has suddenly popped up in outlet stores all across Swabia. *Why, in order to succeed, one has to follow the footsteps of the many that have forged a similar path. Sometimes, it is simply about knowing when to leave, when and how to take one's bow.* Lord Burlington's recent lecture is still on everyone's mind. No, he is wrong, Dr. Honorable decides. The lecture wasn't about the making of sturdy and fashionable gooseberry garments at all. In fact, the lecture was about something entirely different. But it is no matter. I live my life just the way I want to live it. Indeed, I am blessed to have freedom of motion. And if the young people of Cecil's generation just can't see it that way, then so be it. But what am I saying? There is a forest on fire outside the city, just above the heath, and there are millions and millions of ordinary Swabian citizens standing around, gazing at the flames, not lifting a finger to help. It does a person good, thinks Izetta (in a far-off place nowhere near Swabia), thinks Dr. Honorable, thinks Lord Burlington, thinks Tom Terrific, thinks Mr. Jones, thinks every single ordinary Swabian citizen. Swabian fig cigarettes just do a person good.

THE ENEMY DECIDED TO STUDY ITSELF SCIENTIFICALLY.

If the enemy looks at itself face to face does that mean it will also turn on itself, become an enemy to itself? Or will it become its own ally? The problem, of course, is not in our hands, not ours to answer. The enemy may see itself, or it may not, but that is, of course, the enemy's choice and not ours. The Blue Ox is chewing on the branches of a gooseberry tree, cutting through its bark, leaving behind walking sticks for travelers to find. She imagines that her enemy is Lord Burlington, or anyone who would not respect her, or anyone who would take advantage of her, or try to hurt her, or anyone who would keep her where she does not want to be. That is Lord Burlington to a tee. The Blue Ox is nomadic. She remembers living on his estate. It's so unnatural to live in the same place all the time. The smell of the sulphur in the mansion, and all the dying things there, and the melon rinds lying out on a dish by the pool, impress upon her nose from memory. But in the field outside, under the sun and among the dog orchids and spider orchids, you are sort of at home, although not completely at home. This is what she thinks. Because this lifestyle, lying out in a field, also feels like a kind of resort-style living. And then you have to get out of here because life has to have just the right amount of struggle attached to it. I live my life just the way I want to live it, she thinks. But one of her lithe blue sons, trotting beside her, reads her thoughts with perfect agility. For they communicate in pictures, as all blue oxen do. But how do we know that we want anything that we think we want? And who is we, anyway? says the tiny little calf. His skin is as blue and silver and as smooth as a dolphin's. He looks like he belongs in the ocean—or to the ocean, molded into the coruscating waves themselves, molded into underwater glass. The son of the Blue Ox is a dynamic and ever-changing figure. He moves like the darting weeds of the sea. He is not fully formed yet. Still he is here and he's been born. And the Swabian hills are so beautiful this time of year, and there hasn't been a landslide in years. But then he hears limericks in his head (Swabians of course are famous for their limericks) and he gets distracted.

There once was a bucket of fire,
a gazebo, some blood, and a squire.
The squire bled blood.
The blood made the fire.
And fuck you, Lord Burlington, you liar!

There once was a man with disease.
His gout, his dropsy, his fleas.
He said, Where's the cure?
Why is life so impure?
Dr. Honorable, prescribe me my poison now, please!

Now it's impossible to tell what the enemy truly is: whether it is his mother's problematic assertion (her claim that she truly approves of the state of her life when she's obviously choosing an anachronistic/nomadic lifestyle in an urban/agrarian world), or is it the ground beneath him shifting, or is it time, or is it the war, or is it disease, or is it his vulnerability to physical harm, or is it his ability to get distracted so easily after all, succumbing to election year rhetoric. I have to get out of here, he thinks. My home suddenly feels strange. And he's noticed that his mother has seen something she likes. A bit of gooseberry-flavored syrup dripping off of a canary orchid. She is off to consume it, to stick out her long blue tongue. Fine traveling companion you are, he thinks, and now she has become the enemy again, somewhat. We were better off before the war, before all the death and all the destruction. Before the world was torn to bits. We were much better off. The little bull is truly a fighting man. He is small but stubborn, wiry but gilded by his own strength. He finds that he does not believe anything anyone says about anything. But he listens. He is a good listener. And he is cautious. He hears the language with his ears, all the blows it deals, the heathen idioms. He takes it like a man. Like a detective. He knows there has to be a winning truth. A side to believe in. And he's smart enough to know that he should always have enemies, and the quest is to make your enemies into your allies (because what are enemies, anyway, but *triggers for your own pain?*). He knows that the world is designed antagonistically and hypocritically and paradoxically and competitively: there is health, and there is disease, and they stem from the same source. The sun rising over the hills, brightening the fire. The fire on the face. He knows that diseases are not meant as punishments. But thankfully, he knows that because of disease, there are also doctors, and there is also medicine... in order that we may learn the reasons that things are the way they are... in order that we may learn that all our knowledge is nothing... in order that we may know that all things function in their own time, and do not bend to our desire and will. In order to know that what we desire may not actually be quite good for us after all. In order to know what we are like when we are healthy. The fire is burning again in the hills. Taking the shape of a beehive, a flaming, scorching palindrome, a flaming, scorching paradox: a symbol divided and classified into four parts. There is a threat now to the endangered Swabian mollusk. Its shells are starting to thin, and then everything will be tossed into turbulence and chaos. The enemy is all around now, so much so that I cannot recognize it from anything else. Where does it stop and start? Is the world falling to bits or not? Can't you all see that unless we do x,y,z, a,b,c and d,e,f, and h,i, j, we will all die? Can't all of you agree with my position? If you don't agree with me, does that make all of you the enemy? Or is this a pleasant day after all. Perhaps I am home after all. He is lost among his thoughts. And either he is or isn't lost. Or he has lost to his thoughts and his thoughts have won. To triumph is a strange concept entirely. We were better off before the war.

THE DURATION SOUGHT OUT TO STUDY THE NATURAL AND CHASTISEMENT SCIENTIFICALLY.

But to belong to something makes all the difference in the world. It causes us to turn into things. Or it causes us to not be things. The way of the world is a piece of pound cake. It is important to listen. Turning your ear to the turnip patch, to the gooseberry bushes. A person makes a mistake turning away from love. *Dr. Honorable at your service.* And the gooseberry bushes on the Burlington estate are ready. And the trees and the grass and the moss on the meadow are ready. And everything is ready and nothing hurts because, for once, it is time. There are rutabagas on Lord Burlington's estate, and the colors of the raindrops as they fall are dramatically different. And it is that time of year again, but no one pays attention because of the color, because of how things look on the surface. In fact, everyone notices one thing or another and these are easy, breezy days on the Burlington estate and in the country and provinces of Swabia in general. There is a Book lying on the ground and Lord Burlington knows the Book and knows every page in the Book by heart. The Book is gold and beautiful, embossed with one kind of genuine imitation synthetic material or another. Lord Burlington would eat the Book if he could. He would pick the Book up in his hands and just tear it to pieces and eat the Book all up, if he could, that is. If the Book wasn't so bloody valuable, thinks Lord Burlington. If it didn't cost so damned much to have printed, embossed, and translated. And whoever left my Book on the ground will have to answer to me! And where is that blasted Cecil anyway? I saw him just a few minutes ago rolling one of those blasted fig cigarettes, and he'd better pick up the butts and he'd better clean up the ashes, too... It is time for Tom Terrific to go. He has been in Swabia, he believes, for too long. And the Swabian coast will look nice and the water will feel good when it reaches his feet, and he will be in control again. Can't you come to *our* house for once? says the Blue Ox. You are really missing out on something if you don't come over to our house once in awhile and listen to our music. We oxen can sing up a storm. The Ox is big and blue and beautiful and there is nothing like it in all the forests of Swabia. I could make you something to eat. I could even make you a cookie if you were in the mood for something sugary and sweet. I could even make you something nice to wear. Galoshes, or, perhaps, a multi-colored gooseberry coat. I can sew too. And with that the Blue Ox laughs, or seems to be laughing behind its giant burgundy eyes.

A FEEBLE ATTEMPT AT HARMONY SOUGHT OUT TO STUDY A FEEBLE ATTEMPT AT MATRIMONY SCIENTIFICALLY.

Dr. Honorable approaches the estate of Lord Burlington on his own two feet. His coat is purple, as well as his feather, and his hat. He is thinking of marriage, in an untangled sense. He is thinking of marriage because it is a day of pleasant weather; the vaulted blue sky is sifting through the healthy grass, as if, as if…the sky were sand and the grass were…as if, as if… and as if the grass were… never clumped, or fibrously tangled, or a triad of wa-ter-waste, plant-waste, and poison—a sieve. And the lawn is fit for a king or a rich man or woman. There is a tennis court and a fish pond and a gazebo and a pool, as well as many other features. It is a good time on the Lord Burlington estate. And the outside, the outdoors, feels safe, because today is so free from blemishes, my body is so free from blemishes, and I am so free from bodily discomfort! I could be outside but feel locked alone inside a room at the same time. Today I can feel full of steady comforts. I never have to shrink my spirit today. The day is so nice I might as well be in an echo chamber, in an image box. Today is a nice day after all. *Dr. Hon-orable at your service...* What kind of service? Aren't you out of a job these days? says Lord Burlington, laughing. He is in his blue velvet waistcoat and lifting the glass jar off the rose at the back of the house. Lord Burlington treats the glass as if it were made of some kind of precious material, and the rose, for good or bad, is like family. Dr. Honorable grabs a small handful of baby chives from the back garden, and a handful of edible thistles, and takes a seat in a reclining chair beside the fish pond. The orange fish all have fevers. They are agitated and fanning their tails recklessly and making ghastly but beautiful bubbles. The air is orchid scented and gooseberry scented and apple scented, and the estate is creaking all over with the ghost of Samantha. Despite her slightness Samantha fills the whole house. She plants steambug daisies in the hallway, leaves behind trails of coarse aluminum and apple rinds. She is tapping her feet on the hard wood, on the marble, on the stone walls, unclipping a gold barrette. She is all echoes. She is formed but not fully formed; dead and soon to be born. Some strands of her hair have fallen on the floor. Besides, there is something that she wants. But Dr. Honorable pulls out his pockets to reveal that they are empty. This is, one supposes, a gesture of good faith, of a self-proclaimed honest man, of masculine vulnerability. Dr. Honorable notes the good taste of Burlington's choice of curtains. Red and not too dusty, good for catching things, good for holding the scent of the room. Today Dr. Honorable has brought curatives for dropsy and depression. What was that you said? says Dr. Honorable, fishing for a pen. I said what kind of service are you here to execute? Lord Burlington snuffs, checking his vocal timbre. One supposes this is a gesture of controlled superiority. For those who can control, or be in control, must be superior. Burlington is a fighting man, and terrible at concealing it. He always wants something after all; always wants to possess as many precious materials as he can. Gold, good books, rare fish that are easy to maintain, fantastical formulae that are past and done with, herb gardens with the impervious purple lemon balm and the fruit orchids of post-war Swabia, the Crown Jewels of the forlorn regency of post-war Swabia, the blue diamond-encrusted Shield of post-war Swabia, all the cotton, all the fig tobacco, all the rice, all the paper. The truth is *something* after all. A piece of pound cake. An untranslated Book. Well, says Honorable, laughing, there are two kinds of services I could technically and realistically accomplish, as there are two kinds of Physicians. He wishes to be in charge again. He wishes to demonstrate that being in charge is just something he knows how to do. But it all depends on whether I have faith in you; that is, what kind of faith the physician has in the sick. Do you think I am sick? says Lord Burlington, laughing. He is sitting cross-legged and sipping a strawberry lemonade and flapping away a small bee with his sleeve. Well, says Honorable, we all know what the Swabian coast can do to a man's spirit. And besides, a person always makes a mistake turning away from love. At this statement Lord Burlington pours his drink on the ground and clamps down in a grizzly manner on some ice, his teeth fully bared, his eyes reflecting an image of black flags. It is important to listen! adds the Doctor. What is there to listen to, really? says Burlington, laughing. What really? The sound of outdoor markets? The sound of you? The sound of the wind? The sound of the people? The rutabagas and the turnips and the things underground and the color of the rain this time of year? To the sound of the want of something? The want for something? He is ready, once more, to fight with words. To war a little bit oddly in his way. But the Doctor is unruffled. In fact, Honorable unlaces his shoes and takes off his socks and bares his feet in the pleasant wind. The sky looks sated, like a full blue stomach. It is all very pretty. Everything in existence sends messages, even if they do not speak in words. And I can cure you with medicine, or by faith, says the Doctor, But it isn't your faith I'm concerned with. Whether I can work miracles really depends on my faith in you. But first you must admit that you are sick.

THE PAST ATTEMPTED TO SCIENTIFICALLY STUDY THAT WHICH WAS FORMULAE.

I'm putting my arms around you again in the shed, or in the barn, Tom Terrific said one fine morning to his new girlfriend Esmeralda. I am putting my arms around you again because the world is great and big and because there are very many things one can do here, and, besides, it is always today, and always just the way you want it to be, but if, and only if, you let the day carry you. But a Blue Ox is never special. And I will never be special again. Unless you milk her, of course, says Lord Burlington, and you can if you wish. Lord Burlington says this because he is not at all nice, and he gets to say this because everyone, at this point, is standing on his land, and understands this fact, and therefore accepts the situation as it is. It takes a long time to get into things anyway, and I don't care. I am not, after all, prejudiced, adds Lord Burlington. Lord Burlington is standing on his estate and the world is green and the sky is blue and it is a fine day all up and down the Swabian coast. And just because you are standing on my estate doesn't mean that you have to be what you have to be. You are still perfectly free to become something else, if that is what you truly wish. And, in fact, there is a dream still in Tom Terrific's mind. And the dream is utterly consuming and all powerful. Tom Terrific is standing in a barn and putting his arms around a Blue Ox. A dandy Blue Ox. A real fine Blue Ox. A sweet as anything Blue Ox. He is putting his arms around her. And Tom Terrific is having his dream while Lord Burlington lectures and while the spider in the alley spins its web. And, somehow, the whole story is most disturbing. The way the story moves from one place to another. And I was dreaming, says Tom Terrific. And I was dreaming, and then I heard you talking, Esmeralda. At this point, there is nothing left in the barn. In fact, it has been millions and millions of years since the land in that part of the Swabian central coastal plain has been used for farming. There are illegal crops being grown, of course, millions and millions of illegal crops being grown at any given time, and this is, in fact, what has brought Tom Terrific to this place. There is the thought of easy money, or easy profit, in Swabia these days. The post-war boom economy is in full flower. But you almost let me say it this time, whispers Esmeralda. She is standing on the grassy meadow and has two or three or four large rings around her body. The rings float, are suspended in the air by some unknown, unknowable, unseen, unseeable, force. My mouth was open, my lips were ready to move, and I was about to say it for the first time. What did you say, my dear? asks Lord Burlington with a smile. The secret, of course, grins Esmeralda, but I was not talking to you. I have never spoken to you in my whole life. I have never yet said a word to you, and I never would and never will. But you are my Lord, or not my Lord at all, adds the spider, spinning its web. There are very powerful post-war economic boom forces at work in Swabia at that time. And one can try and hide from them. Or one can run around in circles and dawn all sorts of disguises. One can do what has been done millions and millions of times before. For example, one can put a head up on the wall, a favorite head, if you will. Your head, your head. Put your head, your favorite head, for example, on the barn wall. And then one will surely take his rightful place among the pitchforks and harnesses and plows and sticks and spurs, thus, and simply, among every device for torture ever constructed by human beings. And this because... And this because... And this because... But you are being rather judgmental, says Lord Burlington. Still, remember, that you are, in fact, allowed to be what you wish to be in this time and place. Because this is, in fact, only an entrance. Why, here, let me demonstrate what I mean. And, at that, Lord Burlington does a dance. He dances in a circle, and his dance, in a sense, becomes the end of things, or rather, the beginning of the end of things. What you want from me is form, Lord Burlington screams. He has forgotten that he is dancing to music that only he can ever hear. What you really want from me is a happy mistake, and this is something I can give to you, Esmeralda, that is, if, and only if, you tell me your secret…

THE UNION OF RESEARCHER AND OBJECT SOUGHT OUT TO STUDY THE WRONG SIDE SCIENTIFICALLY.

Esmeralda has found that she's become addicted to fig cigarettes. She flicks them out of her windowsill at dusk and the ashes fall with no weight, like they were strings of broken spiderwebs. Weightless, like red socks. They fall because of the existence of broken spiderwebs. The union of researcher and object jots this image down. Tom Terrific says that he does not understand the concept of addiction. He believes everything is a choice. Why here, says Esmeralda, then let me demonstrate the concept to you. The union of researcher and object crouches secretly in the corner of her one-bedroom apartment and observes with great anticipation. It is green, it is red, it is purple, it is yellow, it is pletchy, it is divine, etc. It believes that Esmeralda has a grain of truth to reveal. It feels what she feels. Gloomy, full of urges, and full of hope. However, it has not taken sides in the argument yet. There is still not enough information to go on, but there will be soon—of that, it is confident. Tom stands up in the living room and observes Esmeralda. He is upright and wears a belt of just the right width and length. It is a perfectly fitted, very fashionable belt. But he is tense today. There are too many thoughts in the world to consider. There are too many ways a career can go wrong, a body can go wrong. Just think of the teeth alone. The gums. There is too much giving and not enough receiving. He stands as if he holds many meadows in his fists, but this time his fists are clenched, as if he could crush fire. Esmeralda walks barefooted to her refrigerator and peers inside. Her arms rummage around, then her body makes a movement that indicates she sees something she likes. Of this, the union of researcher and object makes note. It also notes the colorless gardenia water inserted behind her ear. She takes out a small crate of gooseberries that she purchased at the infamous Swabian outdoor market. It is held every Monday and Wednesday and specializes in a great variety of wholly legal and allowable crops. You can buy dandelions and dog orchids and heirloom fruit orchids and watercress and limeade and roma tomatoes on-the-vine and sweet milk from a Blue Ox and her daughters. And, of course, as many hand-rolled fig cigarettes as you can stomach. The best in the world. The blue oxen are easy to seed these days, because the weather is so pleasant, the barleygrass so green, and all sensible creatures (man not included) possess seeds for their own propagation. This means that all creatures (man not included) like foliage, like grass, like stone and ore, like the planets, like a pest, like a moth, like a fragment or swath of medicine, are self-mothering. But here we are exclusively concerned with man. Because we should only be concerned with man. There is no one as great as man. No one as unique, as special, as man. No one as smart as man, or as good with inventions, philosophies, and tools. And all other substances are but crude envelopes. And all other substances are but potential for death and disease (and consequently for remedies). Of course, if you took the other side, you would have to advocate a new approach to nature. Tom Terrific either does or does not advocate a new approach to nature. He is wearing a fine straw hat and he is watching Esmeralda crouch low to dig inside her refrigerator. She still has not found the item she is looking for. She is acting as if... as if... he has already forgotten the question. He is thinking of the hill, of the wide meadow, of many fragrant meadows, he is thinking of leaning up against a gooseberry tree, he is thinking of his Acting Mayor of All Swabia office, he is thinking of everything and everyone that is not in the room with him at this moment. A person is truly sick if they turn away from love. A person will be addicted until they can be who they are supposed to be simply by virtue of being born. He begins to dream, and becomes consumed by his dream. The dream is consuming him mentally, utterly. And this, of course, the union of researcher and object finds to be problematic. It cranes its neck a little bit, for it cannot decide whether man would rather consume his dream, or be consumed by his dream. This would of course lead to very different outcomes. It might even lead to a new approach to nature. A new approach to the thought of easy money, of easy profit, of easy entanglement, of easy death, of easy manipulation, of easy manipulation in a lab, of easy separation of all that should be joined. A new approach to every torture device ever created by human beings. A new approach to gambling. A new approach to love. A new approach to marriage. A new approach to eating, fashion, and work. A new approach to illness. After all, we are discussing man here, we are concerned with man here, man is of utmost importance, and therefore such things must be brought in as evidence. Esmeralda finds what she has been looking for. It is tucked away at the back of the refrigerator, beneath the horsesauce and the horsetomatoes and the rutabagas and half-cut green peppers. She takes the little tornado in her hand. It is small, so small, barely a vortex, and whirling around its invisible center. I almost forgot that I had bought this. Thank goodness, or else it would have gone bad. First its core would have collapsed. And that's not a good thing, believe me, she says out loud. Soon she plans on eating it, and then soon it will become a part of her. She is the weather, a hurricane. It is right for weather to feed on weather. And we don't want our hurricanes addicted to cigarettes, even those produced from a good legal crop of fig tobacco. However, to demonstrate her point to Tom, Esmeralda makes a sacrifice. She breathes hard and the little cyclone withers in her hands. It dies like a purple spider going to sleep, closing its eyes. I've killed it without eating it—now do you believe me about my addictive nature? she asks. Tom Terrific does not know what to say. And the union of researcher and object is also perplexed and silent. It does not know which side to take. For they do not know whom Esmeralda is addressing the question to—itself, Tom Terrific, the little dying cyclone, or her very self.

THE INSENSIBLE CREATURE ATTEMPTED TO SCIENTIFICALLY STUDY THE SEED.

Floating above a hilltop will get you nowhere. Come down from there right this minute, Cecil! And housing. And planting coconut trees. And staring in the mirror. And fixing yourself drinks. And asking a lot of foolish questions. You should have taken a boat. You should have brought a bottle of gooseberry wine, just in case. You should have become more or less what you were going to become just by virtue of your having been born. And this is tomorrow, and tomorrow will come, but you do have to listen. There has been no rain in Swabia for an entire season. There has been no rain, and still there is no place to go. You have to take a short walk to a coastal plain and get lost and tear the ends of things into millions and millions of pieces if you want to make any progress. You have to pay your way and live in dark holes and then command Swabian naval vessels and look for all the ways one can to make one's estate even more profitable. You have to be that which you are not and never will be. It is beautiful here in the morning, says Lord Burlington to Cecil. He is sitting at a table with two glasses and a vintage bottle of gooseberry wine. The wine, as advertised, is good for any occasion. And this, though an advertising slogan, is as true today as it was yesterday and as it will be again tomorrow. You are turning yellow, the color of a daisy. You are turning red and green, and providence has been kind to you, but you have to do a better job of listening and being responsible and saving for a rainy day. It is always like this on the Swabian coast when the rain has stopped for the longest time, for an entire season, in fact, and the people are more and more disorganized and more and more in love with the idea of magic and the idea that magicians will come and free them from all their problems. Still, it was Mr. Jones's idea to come there in the first place, and thus everyone is there. In fact, there are millions and millions of people there. Why, it seems that people will follow Mr. Jones anywhere these days! Esmeralda is Mr. Jones's daughter, and she is a hurricane, and she has come to that place, too, and with fresh acorn bread for lunch, and because she is afraid of what she knows but never sees, she laughs and hates the very idea of a car. But it is dead here in this place and I am dead and self-absorbed and I copy everything I see and it is always this way when the rain stops for good, and, for the life of me, I don't know what the problem is, thinks Mr. Jones. I can't figure it out. I think I will start an investigation. Oh, but how it bothers me today that I am dead and not good for anything. *Dr. Honorable at your service.* And this is getting old, thinks Dr. Honorable. This complaining and bewilderment on the part of Mr. Jones is getting me down. It is important, critical even, for Mr. Jones and everyone else to remember that Dr. Honorable is, in fact, a doctor and not at all a magician. This *is* getting shiteously boring, but soon things will take an interesting turn, I'm sure, says Dr. Honorable to Mr. Jones. Dr. Honorable does like that he doesn't have to mind his bedside manners as much when he's treating Mr. Jones. Mr. Jones is dead and is, therefore, less sensitive than some of the Doctor's other patients. Soon things will indeed be on solid ground again, Jones, you'll see. Dr. Honorable gives Mr. Jones a big smile and a reassuring pat on the knee and begins, inadvertently, to sing an old song: *I was working as a waitress in a cocktail bar, that much is true...Don't, don't you want me?... Don't you want me, baby?* Still, it is sad, the song, the way Honorable has made it, is sad, as sad... as sad... and Mr. Jones's real medical concerns are sad, too, and it's all true and not at all well and good and it is never going to be well and good, and that is true, too, and that's what Lord Burlington thinks, and that's what Mr. Jones thinks, and that's what every ordinary Swabian citizen thinks, or did think, once, when there was, actually, more reason to be hopeful.

LUST sought out to study THE TASK OF THE PHYSICIAN scientifically.

Izetta, wearing nothing but her cream-colored slip, is opening the alleyway closet again. Her shoulders and her feet are bare and she is searching for some lip balm. She notices everything in the closet. An umbrella, a flashlight, two hangers, vacuum cleaner attachments, a vase, a gooseberry coat, a shoebox, fire, water, earth, air, ether, medicinal spray, an old vial, an old cure, garters, an old way of thinking, and a pair of new shoes. And she finds a picture. Not only of the blue Swabian coast, but of the man on the sand. He is wearing velvet swimming trunks. They have a tight elastic band that ripples around his tanned pelvis. She knew him once. If only I could believe that Swabia was more than just an idea, she thinks to herself, sighing. Her heart is open again. It is red, it is purple, it is green. She rubs the picture in an erasing motion with her thumbnail. It is getting old, this complaining and this bewilderment and this loneliness and this longing and this longing to be touched. Izetta looks at the picture of the man on the sand and she feels desire, feels the humour of her heart. His skin. My skin. I am someone who cares about others, she thinks. She suddenly feels pangs of hunger and of thirst. She is craving healthy green foods: weeds like sorrel and purslane and dandelions and feeble little fruit orchids. Dying plants are always her favorite. She does not know whether her strain of sympathy is the unhealthy kind, as it draws her to sick and often overlooked things, like the one plant in a nursery that shouldn't be purchased. The weak seeds that have little chance. She grabs the ladle in her hand and enters the kitchen and stirs the stew. The celery has been added, and Mr. Jones will be over soon. He will put his hat on the hook beside the door.

He will make expert, starchy tugs at his pants to straighten the stripes of his suit. She thinks to herself, as she stirs the pot, I am neither dead nor selfish, nor do I copy everything I see. I am real and I am kind and I am hopeful. I need to remind myself, occasionally, that I am alive. I am alive! And she has memories, many of them. She remembers lying on the sand in very pleasant weather, when the stars looked as if… as if they were palms of virtue, sweet baskets of rye, telltale signatures of purple spiders…and there was the time the sails of the ships of the Swabian navy were cold and thrashing. A gentle hurricane was on the horizon. She and the man in the velvet swimming trunks had a bottle of some of Swabia's finest gooseberry wine pressed from a very good legal crop of berries. They even drank from glasses made out of very precious materials. The man in the memory is not acting like an odd-lot intellectual, or an architect, or someone who patents seeds for profit, or an overly focused layabout, but rather like a man acting upon his attraction. He lies lengthwise on the sand and tips up his glass and attempts to look into Izetta instead of *at* her. He says, you know, there are a great number of very many things we can do here. Izetta thinks to herself, I have two choices: I could respond to the world as it is, or I can act as if I already live in the world that I desire—that I imagine will come to be. And my imagination is rich in things that are like seeds and I know what desire, his desire, my desire, means. And I know that men get kindled by physical appearances, and women too. And what I do now all depends upon my will. She decides to act as if she does not live in the world as it presently exists but to act as if she lives in the world as she wants it to become. *Dr. Honorable at your service…* And this is still relevant, sadly, because there is still much illness and much discomfort and much need for physicians and general improvement. There are real medical concerns, and real bodies too, and other maladies. And people are really alive. Izetta tells the Doctor that she feels unified, within and without, and therefore to please let her make her own decisions, her own mistakes. Dr. Honorable agrees: I am a Doctor and not an ass, he sniffs, laughing, but adds: I will take my medicine bag and sit there far away from the shore, by a little dune. If you need me, just holler. I have many instruments at the ready. As the Doctor walks off unsteadily, leaving footprints in the dank, coral sand, Izetta takes in a deep breath and feels her body heave and coalesce like a diamond. She looks at the man lying on the beach and digs in under his velvet swim trunks. She has heard, and knows, that they each carry half a seed, and that together they could become whole. As their red lips exhale and compress and press into each other's she knows that there is an attractive force and seed drawing seed unto itself, like amber or a magnet. And her will has determined to do this and now she feels a force rising up from the humours of her heart, her liver, her spleen, her bones, her marrow, her blood, her blood vessels, her muscles, her flesh, and all that is her body. And when any two bodies draw together they can create one seed. But here on the coast, here in the moment, and here beneath the tiled roofs waving their black flags, there is no place for him in her all-consuming dream for the world. They are not unified. And knowing this, she feels as a jolt. She feels her body riveted, moving too fast, like a car, as if it were a weapon, a sudden hooked sliver, her heart sliced. The Physician is quick to reply. *Dr. Honorable at your service…*

AMBER OR MAGNET ATTEMPTED TO SCIENTIFICALLY STUDY THE MATRIX, OR THE SEED.

You are my best friend, Burlington. You know that. And not only because you live on the central coastal plain of Swabia, though I do enjoy coming here and visiting you and getting to stay on your beautiful estate... You were very good looking when you dressed in gooseberry and spent sufficient time on your appearance. And now all we have to show for our labors is seed and selling things at half price at various Swabian outlet malls, and I swear, Cecil, it is hot today. However, the labors become us... We are spelling our names wrong. There is something wrong in the kitchen. I must get up and look at what the rutabagas and turnips are doing on the grill and, all in all, it has been a very good day. Why, it is as if... as if... I am on my way to a Swabian outlet mall and I am running out of money and I am at the end of my rope and I must think of an inexpensive gift idea for Lord Burlington's upcoming Platinum Sapphire Initiation Ceremony. It is almost spring and I like to stay prepared. Funny, I look down and there are more than one of them by my feet. There are so many seeds. I have to live at least a day in order to see where the seed will land tomorrow. I want to have lunch with Lord Burlington. I want to wash my feet. I am hungry and I don't want to be sad or become less than myself in order to sell my wares. I will wash my feet when I return home and Lord Burlington will find me just getting out of the tub, and there will be no guilt. It is the color of a stone. Or the horseberries and horsetomatoes and all the new seed that has come into being since the time Lord Burlington hired Cecil to plant his very first garden... There is someone in the alley. And there is a Blue Ox on a grassy meadow. It is a Blue Ox that will carry the seed to the places that Tom Terrific goes.

There is no coercion, and there is no enemy, not an enemy in sight. But the bit of amber embedded in Tom Terrific's front tooth shines in the sun and there is only a little way to go before he reaches the outlet mall. The invisible is visible, and it is real, too, shouts Lord Burlington. You have to remember that, and you have to keep a healthy distance from the flame when you are grilling fresh rutabaga and turnip. And there is no turning back now, not since that boy came to the outlet mall with those damned gooseberries and horsetomatoes and homemade horsesauce. But I have to get my seeds back. I know he stole them from me. I will get that boy yet. Why, when I get my hands on that boy... But what I've been meaning to tell you for a long time is to take everything in moderation. Oh, excuse me, *Dr. Honorable at your service...* And what I have found after examining this—the plant, the stone, the seed, the Book, the work being done—is that the project is nothing short of my long-awaited new translation of the *Bible of the Species.* But you are being dull and competitive and deceitful. You are a liar, Burlington. No one has taken your seeds away. You should really be punished for making slanderous accusations like that. Still, there is something attractive in the way you walk, or rather, your gait, the way you carry yourself. There *is* something nest-like, so to speak, a nest-like quality, and vacant, and, well, scary about you, in general, but we have known each other for a very long time, and I was not born to criticize you. You broke my heart. You took everything to its worst extreme. I came here to purchase a loaf of gooseberry bread, to beg your pardon, to get on my hands and knees and pray, to look for love in all the wrong places... However you wish, I have been met with resistance before. Why, you are supposed to be my best friend, Samantha, and all you ever do is criticize me.

THE CAR SOUGHT OUT TO STUDY THE MOUNTAIN SCIENTIFICALLY.

There was a car on the lone central coastal plain of Swabia. It was the first and only car. It was driving down the road and cranking smoke and loud music. It was blue. Lord Burlington saw the car as a precious commodity and desired it. He thought it would make a good holiday present for himself. But who was there to give it to him? He was starting to view himself painfully and pitifully, like a kind of dull survivor. The rose at the back of the house had retreated for the winter. Its stalk and stem were looking thorny, brown, and ribbed. Everything in the garden was sloping down. Of course, Lord Burlington could have been perceiving everything through the false lens of self-loathing. As a result, Samantha had not haunted the mansion on the estate for days. There was no smell of gorse, no smell of sulphur, no horsedressing. Her footsteps, walking sideways up the walls, shaking the mansion, rattling the shingles, had been absent. Lord Burlington is baring his head to the elements. And when did everything turn into such a swirl, a haze of opinions and failures? He thinks to himself: perhaps I should plant some new seeds. He thinks to himself: I am running out of things to buy. The car drives and treads down the lonely road. There is not an enemy in sight. And the mountain knows it has very few enemies and is not sure yet whether or not the car is one. The car is small and has a kind of dull color, a relentlessly bad devious blue, and is kind of fragile, despite its metal armor. It's nothing that would survive in nature. The mountain knows why it is called a mother and a father and a generator and a forgiving entity. The mountain knows why it is called a microcosm. It is made up of seeds and a combination of seeds that cannot be replicated anywhere else. This is not coercive. Samantha whispers into Lord Burlington's ear while he is asleep and while he is dreaming of having everything and everyone in the world in its proper place (that is his all-consuming wish, or dream): you are very good looking when you dress in blue (she whispers to him), in that gooseberry coat, in that horsehair vestment, in that pair of twill socks, in that gold naval clasp, in nothing but that Swabian flag horsetowel, in that crested navy ring, in that tomato-branched mustache, in that diamond-studded bang flip, in those water-chestnut lounge trousers, in those feathered-sapphire galoshes, in that sterile peacoat. You are very good-looking when you are naked. Lord Burlington turns in his sleep and dreams he is drag racing his new car. But he dreams that he is racing against himself, and no one else. The worst kind of competition, really, or the best, or the most innocuous, depending on your point of view. It's a tough call. But he sees no one as a formidable enemy—a formidable challenge to himself—but himself. Is this a form of loneliness and comfort? His wealth is preposterous after all. The wind is rattling the hair on his head. He turns in his sleep and in his all-consuming dream his hands reach out for a recipe, the right one, but if only he knew what it was he wanted to eat. But you would like to think that man (and we are talking about man here) would have no enemies if there were only one kind of people and each person looked and acted like the other. You would like to think that. And you forget the concept of a self divided against itself, or a very abstract thought eating itself to bits. If there was just one kind of person, then there would be no matrix in which to properly place each organ, each brain, each head, each eye-crystal, no carpenters building proper houses for people to live in. In other words, there would be no mountain. And that is why man, when composed, when created, must be born out of two people and not just one. If man were born of the seed of just one individual, then no other form of man could grow. This is also true of earth's other contents: walnut trees, for example, or orchids, or walking sticks, or the endangered Swabian mollusk, or spiders. There can be no two mountains that are alike. I mean, come on—it was never that way. Everything in its proper place will shift according to the plan of the mountain. And everything will keep shifting. And Samantha whispers to Lord Burlington in his sleep, she is standing invisibly within the gilded mirror and she is whispering and she means to speak to him out of love: *Buy yourself the car for Christmas and do not worry about your safety. Your nest egg is in plain sight and there is safety all around.*

THE WALNUT TREE SOUGHT OUT TO STUDY THE SEED SCIENTIFICALLY.

I was telling that fool, Cecil, to go and get me a drink of water. You've got the secret ways in and out of this estate all set up and mapped out, don't you, Burlington? But it has gone on too long. What has gone on too long? Tom Terrific asks. I need to know what you know and there is no telling what that means. It is what it means and there is no difference and you take your pencil and your Book and your gardenia seeds everywhere you go. It goes to your house. It goes in your Book. But you've lost the guardian spirit. You've lost the trial and the whole war, too, you idiot. And there is a gazebo on fire on Lord Burlington's estate. Tom Terrific has seen it all before, from above and below. It is a wire on crutches. I'm telling you, Burlington, the estate is crippled now, hopelessly haunted. You have overplowed or over-planted, overplayed your hand, if you don't mind my saying. Why, look at that fish pond, it can barely grow a fish at all nowadays. Lord Burlington is standing with his arms folded, and it is right now, today, and there is to-morrow, but you have to be what you are going to be tomorrow, tomorrow. And it is as if... as if... And that is a temptation I will risk taking, says Lord Burlington to Tom Terrific. Take that walnut tree over there, for example, and the way it grows. Its whole attitude towards living. It is a seed, and we steal seeds and manipulate seeds and then give them back as if they were the same ones we took in the first place, and I am like you and you are like me and we ought to weigh one another's acts, the very weight of our acts, as it were, to prove it. Hey, though, do you really know, what it is to live that way, man? To have to prove it? To always have to prove it? asks Cecil, eating an olive. And Lord Burlington is suddenly a child again and pushes

Tom Terrific to the ground and clicks his heels together and kicks up dust. The way you are attracted to dirt, to dirty things is frightening, shouts Tom Terrific, defiantly. And there is a spider, a very purple spider, who has quite suddenly appeared on the scene. And although the spider cannot speak in words that anyone can understand, the spider is understood perfectly: this talk of the walnut tree, of what is most valuable, of what is right and what is wrong, will only induce pain and suffering and... *Dr. Honorable at your service.* I was asked to come here by a large purple arachnid only recently liberated from a petting zoo. I had to perform eighteen hours of surgery to remove the cotton candy from the spider's abdomen. The surgery was very messy. But the purple can be seen again, and I told the spider that the most important thing to remember is that the purple never really went away. It was and is always there, whether obscured by cotton candy or not. By the way, I hear you are having the Bible re-translated on your estate these days, Burlington? I hear you are paying top dollar for help with the work too. There is a crush of garments. The floor explodes. There is a dangerous sound coming from Lord Burlington's poolhouse. And what is that racket? Lord Burlington asks. It is dangerous and there is dandelion fur and goose-berry and horsesauce everywhere. There is a great tragedy, a disaster, about to take place. And if you need me. If only anyone needed me. You see, this is the story of a walnut tree and a great disaster. You see, this is the story of a Book and the things the Book has to say. You see, this is the story of a life changing experience and the good fortune that could be found, and it was as if... as if... as if... And Lord Burlington begins to sing an old, sad song, but there will be time enough for that, for exploring exactly what that means, tomorrow.

THE BIBLE OF THE SPECIES

AND OTHER

USEFUL CONTENTS, INDICES, AND REFERENCES,

A NEW TRANSLATION,

TRULY TRANSLATED OUT OF THE ORIGINAL TONGUES BY

DILIGENT STUDY,

AND

WITH FORMER TRANSLATIONS INTACT AND DILIGENTLY

COMPARED AND REVISED

ACCORDING TO LORD J. BURLINGTON,

WITH THE AID OF PREVIOUS VERSIONS AND WITH CONSTANT

CONSULTATION OF DIVERSE EXCELLENT LEARNED MEN,

EXPERT IN THE ORIGINAL TONGUES.

SWABIA

11408447

The authorized and revised version conformable to the standard of the

Swabian Paper Mill Society.

1

SAYING SOMETHING
SOUGHT OUT TO STUDY
SAYING NOTHING AT
ALL SCIENTIFICALLY.

There is a gazebo on fire in the rolling hills of Swabia. Did you say you wanted grace? Well, grace will come, but only if you ask for it. Too bad you don't have a father. If you did, you could ask your father for grace. And even if he was stingy about giving it, then at least you would know that you'd tried. Forgiveness? If you had a father, and he was on his deathbed, then you could ask him for forgiveness. You could and you could ask him to forgive you. And even if he didn't forgive you, well, at least you would know that you'd tried. Did you or didn't you just say something? There is a difference, you know, between saying something and not saying anything at all. I can't hear you, Hurricane, says The Ghost, putting

her fingers in her ears. I can't even speak. I can't see straight because it is late and my head hurts and I am thirsty. I am suddenly so thirsty. Hurricane, do you remember when you got those shoes from your father? The ones you're wearing right now? It was Swabian Boat Holiday Day and you opened the box and your eyes got wide. I mean it was impressive, an impressive reaction. Shoes. Your father had given you a pair of shoes. He'd brought the box right into the house. And I would say that you hated. You hated. You didn't take advice. What were you doing anyway? Excuse me, Sir, but I couldn't help but overhear that you were dead, or, excuse me, that was rude, what I meant to say, was that you were drowning. Yes, thank you, says Man. I was just thinking out loud. I have a terrible habit of thinking out loud these days. The house was on fire. No, it was a gazebo. Somewhere, a gazebo was on fire. You, Man, were taking a bath. I was taking a bath, repeats Man. I accuse you, father, you took my shoes, accuses the Hurricane. It was hot, of course, because there was a fire. And I was thirsty. And there is a difference between seeing and not seeing. A slavish dependence on the tides. You could have done a little more to help, you know. You could have helped. Instead you were caught. I saw you. You were caught. I thought you went to get water. The house was burning. No, it was a gazebo. The fire started in the gazebo. We weren't going to have anywhere to sleep that night. And you were busy drowning. I have to admit that, frankly, it was a little disappointing. But, it could have been very different. My father didn't have to give those shoes to me. He could have given me something else entirely. He could have given me something I wanted. And then it rained. And you did die, Man, drowned in field sauce, that time. Or was it folding syrup?

2

THE MOTHERLAND
SOUGHT OUT TO STUDY
THE FATHERLAND .
SCIENTIFICALLY.

One day the Motherland understood that the brain and the heart, and every other organ of the body, were basically like countries or regions, and that they therefore required the right amount of rain, snow, salt, fire, and an ocean, etc., unless they were to fall into chaos and corruption. That which remains balanced in its vitality, compact and harmonious, is vital. And therefore not sick, and therefore never in need of a cure. Yes, it may need the occasional reassurance, occasional words of consolation and empathy, a healthy dose of friendship, of love, and a good night's sleep. Those are, of course, the normal circumstances of maintenance. But the Motherland was feeling that everything and everyone was sick. And

where are you, Tom Terrific, to solve all our problems? She wept often and a lot, crying with fecundity, because she was full of feeling and care, and in summer she rallied herself and sought to nourish all that winter had lost. For example, there were ski boots in the Alps that were forever cracked, there was dried hay, frozen seasides and frozen rooftops, and eroding cliffsides, and the darkness, and the dreaming in the dark, and explorers extending themselves into icy passages. And so she recycled her tears and the soil heated. Everything begins with the soil. It's all about the soil. The soil is the most important thing of all. Now that it was summer and her torso was about to be on fire she prepared for her inquiry into the Fatherland's various positive and complementary attributes: engines and planks, dried apricots, his comforting muscles, all sorts of enhancers and reducers. There are many passages into the Fatherland's body due to his external limbs. But his success as a Fatherland is too reliant on his ability to inspire fear. He is always swinging at his own moving objects, with bats or belts, rockets or shredded marine life, for example, and his sands are too coarse. Do not mistake violence for intelligence, wisdom, or charm. Do not get suckered in. But the Fatherland's talk of probabilities and punishment and threat was all, of course, for show, which the Motherland knew. She taught the Fatherland how to be patient and generous. He learned how not to confuse the Motherland's inquiries with criticism or uncomfortable scrutiny. He bloomed her white flowers shaped like parachutes and half-drooping dog orchids. He sang her songs of virtue and hope so that she could bear all the coldness befalling the hearts of man, including man's threat of death by dissolution. And the songs were quiet and hidden, like a window opening and closing without much noise. He grew crocuses in her metals and made sure she never dried out and was always full of nutrients. And in return she let the spectacles fall from her eyes and, for once, rested. Dear, dear, Motherland, Swabia. Our Swabia. Dear, dear, Swabia. Dear Swabia, our Fatherland. Dearest dearest Swabia.

3

MATH SOUGHT OUT TO STUDY THE WORK SCIENTIFICALLY.

It was always going to be like that. And it wasn't ever going to be any different. Dance around an idea, and then dance some more. And then tell the people things. And a hat was found. And the ground was hard. Math had the answer. The answer fell from the tree. Math read the Book of Life like it belonged to him. The Book of Life did, of course, belong to Math. But it begins to be a bit self-indulgent, thought Math, putting the book down. However, there is something else here. There is something else besides a book in a tree and no one is there to help Man get it down. Man has bad dreams. Man is dead and, alas, cannot have dreams, not in the sense of dreams, or of dreaming. Man, alas, cannot have dreams. No dreams of any kind, i.e., good or bad.

In the end, the gazebo on the Lord's estate is too hot, or too smoky, or there is no air at all. There is a fire. The squirrels and mockingbirds and sparrows and jays are not safe in the trees. And what do people usually think about themselves when they grow up? The Work asked Math one day. Math was looking over a hedge. He was wondering how he would ever get around the fire. And what about the trees? The problem is that possession is often perceived to be the larger and greater part of harmony, of that which is harmonious, and depressing, and it does not pay to analyze, to be Math at all, thought Math. But this problem, this game, is starting to get boring, replied Math. A hat. A shoe. A horse and cart. A breathless moment alone. And you are not alone, thinks Man. Someone else has to be around. Right? The work was going well one night. And it was all by design, by new designs. One day Swabia, even Swabia, will be renewed. And Math was on the grass. And Man was on the grass, or, rather, was the grass. The greater part of that particular patch where Math stood was, in large part, Man. And there was a hat there. And this was before and after the fire, the disaster that started and ended on the Lord's estate. The fire began in the gazebo. There was an Oxen. A tree. And it made Math wonder. The way around one's problems is in, and through, the moment. The second section will begin with a tree.

4

THE LOST KNOWLEDGE OF HER LOST SOCIAL MATRIX SOUGHT OUT TO STUDY SEEDS SCIENTIFICALLY.

Rose wished to plant seeds in the imagination of Woman and Man. Rose was the mother of Woman and Man. Rose was the mother of Man and Woman, and Man and Woman are not seeds, so that they could be free and independent from Nature. However, Rose gave them the use of seeds so they could eat and dream. And in order that they could procreate, she gave them the free will to decide whether they wanted to or not. Rose wished to plant seeds in the imagination of Woman and Man. But Rose designed it so that Man had to decide whether he wanted this seed to grow, and if he decided against it, there would be no seed in him. It is the same with Woman. Rose left her seeds to the free decision of Man. Lost seeds are called heirloom varieties, or Lost Knowledge. Once, Rose was sitting in the back of her house near a tree, sitting quietly in the chair that allowed her to be most like herself. It was wide and comfortable and produced many good thoughts. She was sitting, eating, and trying to think. The Lost Knowledge had been coughing and drifting across meadows of wild barleygrass and sowgrass, tightening its belt. Rose tried to put it in a jar, tried to put its leg in a brace, but that failed. Trying to reclaim, retrieve, understand, make work, make better and not worse: this action would cause Rose to turn red, preparing for battle with her children's disappointing use of free will. She broke straws in half, diced things, tried to get a promotion, took gooseberry tablets, wore clothes with flattering necklines and lots of tactile appeal. She got frustrated, kicked the legs of desks. In some people, the tendency towards war is quick. In others it is slow. And the reddening, battle impulse can begin to swell abnormally, like a wild yam or genetically defective vine, from the feet upwards to the hips, and heart, as far as the eyebrows. Before you know it your heart feels shriveled and bound on a string. This swelling and excessive heat and readiness to fight could be termed excess. Rose still believed she could collect the Lost Knowledge and place it in the sunlight, let it watch the world go by, the cars and cliffs and children, the grass on the sidewalk, a grove of trees, the police sirens, all the animals in the zoo, unhealthy sandwiches (no one appreciates watercress anymore?), and the gates of the old suburbs of Swabia. But the core question being scrutinized is this: there is still the frequency of bodily harm. And there are two kinds of wheat, for example, and two kinds of rice, two kinds of corn, and two kinds of potatoes. And some of these are being manufactured in laboratories and some of these are not. And now Rose is in a precarious position, some may call a trap—hope that the battle has not been fought and lost.

5

WHEAT, FLAX, BARLEY, AND SPELT SOUGHT OUT TO STUDY THE CITY SCIENTIFICALLY.

And Tom Terrific arose early in the morning, made himself a cup of coffee out of strong imported coffee beans, yawned, and looked outside his window. Outside, in the morning, the Physicians were taking up the medicine of primordial MAN. Primordial MAN was at it again, with his inventions and his stories, in other words, all of his best times wrapped up in neat packages. And the earthen Physicians bearing the best blood took the medicine of primordial MAN and patented it continually, and understood how to patent, and patented the blood; and the armed men went before them; and the maladies came after the medicine of primordial MAN was discovered and patented, [the Physicians] blowing with the blood continuously. And up inside the second Air they know the city, and how to build it, and, yea, how to take it down, how to make it unlivable, and how to return it unto the body; so they patented earth's Airs. And if you should feed on the earthen Air, or rise early at the dawning of the Air, and know the city after the same manner in earthen times, then only in that Air will you know the city and earthen times. And you should feed at the earthen time, when the Physicians blow with the blood. And Tom Terrific, feeling at ease, feeling linen, greeting the morning, standing on his porch, said unto the people: 'Shout; for the primordial Lord has given you the city. And the city shall be devoted, even it and all that is thereto, to the primordial Lord...'

6

OVERHEAR ATTEMPTED TO STUDY DON'T HEAR SCIENTIFICALLY.

And this can't be, and it just can't be, said Hurricane. I was reading my book, minding my own business, when something interrupted me. Some noise, or some voice. I think it was the voice of someone I knew once. *I want to get to know you better, Hurricane. I want to get to know you better.* Then there was fire. It was an early day. The Swabian Fire Department would have to come and put out the fire, but things were not that calm. The world was turned to stone. The Hurricane was wearing the shoes that her father had bought for her. They were very special shoes. I could have sworn that your father was wearing the very same shoes, says the Ghost. The Ghost is the Hurricane's best friend. You are wearing a lovely pair of shoes too, Ghost, says

the Hurricane. Hurricane, do you remember that one night, when we stayed up really late, and you were wearing very special shoes, shoes your father gave to you? You were wearing shoes, and the shoes were made of water, to keep you safe, stylish, and comfortable. But you should have purchased a second pair. You could have spent more time with me. But I, of course, make false accusations. I accuse you of all kinds of things, and I turn out not to be your best friend at all. And there is a house on fire. Not quite a house. Rather, it is clear, at this point, that there is a gazebo on fire, somewhere. And there is plenty of water to put out the fire. Tom Terrific has seen to that. He has made sure that the Swabian Fire Department has been sufficiently funded. I saw the water out back by the shed, says the Hurricane. It was in a big bucket. There was plenty of water. Why, it was only the other day. I was drowning in my own momentum. Dying, if you want to know the truth.

I was drowning in my own momentum, out back by the shed and no one came. You were working on your car, Ghost. You were talking to your car. It was maddening. It was the very first time I thought that maybe you were not my best friend after all. Oh, Hurricane. You take things too seriously. You think too much sometimes, I think. Those shoes you are wearing are pretty loud!

7

THE MOST PRODUCTIVE PHASE OF ACTIVITY
SOUGHT OUT TO STUDY
HOME SCIENTIFICALLY.

The Most Productive Phase of Activity owned five large and beautiful, custom-made homes. They possessed some of the best views in Swabia: the black lake, the blue hills spiked with wild grasses, the famous salt pits, the sun rising, the sun setting, the black flags on all the roofs. The houses also had additional attributes that distinguished them from one another. One house was red and had a window to the constellations, one was green and had a view to the financial center (i.e., the natural constitution of human society), one was the color of a sand-dune and had a view towards decay (i.e., downtown Swabia), one was brown like a badger and had a mysterious power over the body and emotions, and the last one was yellow and was very conducive to cooking and introspection. But The Most Productive Phase of Activity was unable to rest and enjoy its own property holdings. It kept dropping its possessions accidentally, like all of its glassware. It still didn't really know what a home was. Was a home something that one owned, or something that one was, something that one carried around, something that one sang to, something that one lied to, something that one shared, something that one coveted, something that one comforted, or something that one used up miserably, and reduced to ashes and splinters? Was a home a mobile or a static thing? Was the primary purpose of a home to provide a space in which one could safely produce a build-up of trash? Honorable Physician at your service, and I am telling you that it is better to have a home that is grounded on solid rock instead of sand. Tom Terrific had just shifted the city ordinances regarding trash. Cans could no longer be thrown out, nor anything toxic, like dried horsetomato vines, nor anything re-usable, like outworn shoes. The Most Productive Phase of Activity hated waste. It hated ill-used time and wasted effort. Perhaps the purpose of home was efficiency? The Most Productive Phase of activity shimmied inside its own spotless scales. If you were to compare it to anything visually, it looked like a perfectly clean, perfectly ordered sack. The Most Productive Phase of Activity loved factories. It loved speed and industry. Needle-making, match-making, pen-making, paper-bag making. Casks of salt, reams of black cloth, bundles of watercress, too-fat-to-fly turkeys. It sank deep into thought. Five houses, really, just wasn't that efficient. Perhaps it was better just to have one? One to be the focus of devotion and ostentatious display? The Most Productive Phase of Activity suddenly felt quite anxious about all that it owned. Felt the burden of its expenditures, its possessions. What should or shouldn't I own? It didn't know if home was something that one owned or something that one was. It didn't know what to do. Perhaps you didn't hear me before, said the Honorable Physician. What informed and experienced creature only desires a doctor who is an outward show? None. Only the stupidest people. A true doctor should practice Virtue, and Astronomy, and Philosophy, and did I say Virtue? Now I've pointed out what is essential in a physician.

8

A NEW APPROACH TO NATURE SOUGHT OUT TO STUDY AN ANCIENT PATHOLOGY SCIENTIFICALLY.

But this had to do with the esoteric. Our story begins with reprimands, no, wait, our story begins in the healthiest region in all heathen Europe: Dalmatia or Salmatia. It was sunset. Tom Terrific could easily see that. The trees in the forest. A new way of dying. No, not dying. He was not dying, not exactly. There was a very beautiful region, Dalmatia or Salmatia, a region considered to be very healthy. And a heart is beating. No, it was not because of the way the heart was beating at that time. It was because of waking up. It was because of the way stories are told. Can you tell me a story? The Ghost asks Tom Terrific. Why, don't mind if I do, replies Tom. And then to dry up. To think, Ghost, that one could actually dry up. I was walking on top of a mountain when I looked down. I parked my car. I needed to take up a hobby, something, anything to take my mind off of my problems. It is wet. No, it is dry. And there is a simple lesson to be learned here. Tom Terrific is leaning on a gate. There are too many messages, and the means of communicating them will become difficult if he's not careful. You will get to where you want to go, Dalmatia or Salmatia, for instance, if you try, says The Ghost. Tom Terrific is trying to communicate, he is trying to tell a story about the rain and the wind and the very first car in all of Swabia. The story continues. You are sitting on the floor and trying to tell your friends good things, good things about themselves. You are educating the masses with your ways and means, with the ways by which you get things done. This, however, does not disperse. There has been no rain in months, in millions and millions of years, which is a very long time. And I asked you once, Ghost, whether or not you could remember the rain. Could you even remember the rain? And the answer was no. Not in a million years. But this is just talking about how we get sick. We talk about how we get sick over and over again. I would rather dance with my cane, get my toenails polished, go to the carwash, visit my friend, live and love and dance and play, as if…and, play as if…and play, as if… But at the back of the house, a Rose. Dalmatia or Salmatia, the healthiest region in all of heathen Europe. A dream of a better life. This makes me mad. The whole world will wish they had taken off their shoes and socks, dipped their feet into the lake. The whole world will wish they had remembered to turn their collars up before they'd gone out into the storm. Then one day it was raining. I was waiting for you. I had asked for something good to happen, and I was waiting for you. You talk on the telephone. The history of this disease. It's an ancient pathology, an esoteric knowledge. What? What's wrong? What did you say was wrong again? I apologize. I was distracted by the sound of something on the roof. I promise I wasn't just thinking of myself. I promise that the thought of a Rose won't consume my kind, the good kind, of thinking about you. I promise that I will go to the healthiest region in all of heathen Europe, Dalmatia or Salmatia? The healthiest place I know.

9

THE TWO SIDES OF CREATION SOUGHT OUT TO STUDY POISON SCIENTIFICALLY.

There was poison, again, in the air, invisibly and in the dust and in the rain, and the air held the people, the world was like a room, and we all know what that means. The Two Sides of Creation were thought to be constantly at war, or at least in constant disagreement, down to the finest points, as when someone cannot decide if a certain sweater is purple or really blue. And it was thought, it was rumored, that The Two Sides of Creation were seeking to study poison with ill intent. In other words, to discover the knowledge that would allow one side to dominate the other, or at least make it very very sick (poison could dole out all of the five great stomach ailments, as well as gout, and muteness, lung-disease,

dropsy?). But really this was not the case. The Two Sides of Creation were not really antagonists. They were never at war and rarely in disagreement. In fact, side A (a.k.a. absolutism) had the finest gooseberry coat, and everyone called it loud, and everyone's emotions were all in a swirl, and everyone was drowning in their own momentum. Everyone that is, except side B (a.k.a. betterment), who had commissioned a coat just as expressive, one made from all the air in all the rooms. Don't even think of the colors. Being made of all the air in all the rooms, it was the only object in the world that could stand still. It was beautiful. And it was a comfort and relief to see one as formidable as side B making the same fashion statement as side A, for no one is immune to peer pressure. Therefore, if A had access to poison, then it certainly wouldn't use the poison on B, even though they might feign an argument. Really, if poison were to be used, it would be used on us. And this can't be, it just can't be, says Ghost. But Ghost, says Hurricane, taking off her shoes. They are special shoes and they are made of water. We can't get smug here with our definitions and newspapers and everything else. And if we are living systems, which we are, then self-organization is the key to our health and stability. Imagine if I was mechanically manipulated to perform a one-dimensional function. Why, I'd be nothing but a crisis, a weapon, or just a very big bucket! Could you imagine that? I could never take care of my own needs, which means my immune system would collapse, and I'd become vulnerable to disease and attack. The Hurricane speaks and there is plenty of water in the room and no poison to be found between two friends. You are my good and true friend, says Ghost, and let us not then argue. No, never argue.

10

THE MOST PRODUCTIVE ACTIVITY SOUGHT TO STUDY THE AIR IN THE ROOM SCIENTIFICALLY.

Talking about it will always get you nowhere. You can bet on that. And suffer. But you've said that before. Because the sun is in the room now and there is trouble. There is trouble here. But you've said that before. And every element belongs in the order of things, but not the social order because that is different and I have no faith in that which that does not belong. But you were fine. You sat there in the room gazing at the marble that had been thrown on the floor haphazardly. You were reading a magazine, a fashion magazine, and there was a trail of crumbs in the way you stopped and stared. But how could you do such a thing? And why were there so many of you? How could you think about what happened out-side the gate and why were so many of your friends, the people you knew and loved, so unhealthy so much of the time? There was a gate of grass. Or bending. Or changing. And what you really want to know is why. Why does this become this and why does that become that and why and what about the falling of the stars and the heads of steam and the men in ties and the marbles and the therapeutic baths and the suffering? Well, lo, the suffering again, and it all leads back to that. You are smart, old man, smart, I tell you. The suffering, your way of thinking about the suffering, your articulation of the suffering will get you everywhere, everywhere with me at least. And at that Man was released, turned into a new man. A store. A sought for principle. And I have found a whole new life in the way I am turned to stone, said Man. I quite like myself this way. I quite like myself the way I've found myself changed around here, wearing a gooseberry coat and stealing my straw-hat and trading my vegetables for everything else I need. But I become too deep when I talk about it. I run the risk of not being solvent at all, of turning into stew or sour candy, or the way you looked at me when I told you that I was all wrong. But my shoes are loud! No, your shoes, sir, have nothing to with it. And, in fact, your penchant, your need, your wish to have a conversation with me at all may have been the very key to your undoing. And you said you were standing at the gate, and you said the story began by a gate made of grass and that one day the people had all turned a pretty shade of blue, and, to clarify, the good kind of blue, and not the bad kind of blue, i.e., not the kind of blue that makes people already dead. But it's already too late to analyze that now, you know.

A CHANGE OF NATURE SOUGHT OUT TO STUDY AN ANCIENT PATHOLOGY SCIENTIFICALLY.

Mr. Jones is back in Swabia and sunning himself gratuitously in the back garden of Lord Burlington's estate. He does not feel quite right. He feels himself in a holding pattern, which is very similar to prison—although nothing is truly similar to prison. Nor is anything truly similar to blood, nor to the intestines and its contents, nor to saliva. Is the body so fragile, so foul, such a great tragedy or disaster about to happen? He stretches out on the sturdy sun-chair and wishes desperately for a mind-altering experience. He does not want to die again this time to make such an experience happen. He does not want to have to feel the floor explode or collapse; he does not want to feel the soil fail or the air drown, he does not want to feel a crush of bones or a crush of garments or a crush of seeds, a crush of shells, a crush of possibility. Too much red. And the horizon is no longer supposed to be toxic. And he thinks of all the new ideas that have come into being since he last died and has at last returned and last consulted the new Burlington translation of the *Bible of the Species*, that is, the Book of Life itself. There was a rumor that Lord Burlington was having the Book of Life translated somewhere on his estate. Supposedly he had tried to conceal the fact that he was performing such very important work, and such very important reality-altering, weather-impacting studies. Studies that began with competing entities: formulae and philosophies about why things were the way they were. Cecil was lying out by the fish pond and sipping on some seltzer water doused with sprigs of mint. He had his sunglasses eased onto the rim of his nose. You know Burlington, man, he says, snapping the elastic band of his velvet swimming trunks. His nails are casually manicured. So the rumors are true about that book of yours. Good for you, Burlington, good for you to be true to your innate nature. To let gossip and rhetoric and representation and reality all coincide. You are precisely as they say, and you are precisely as you see yourself. I find that incredibly reassuring. He runs the mint leaves through his teeth. He dips his fingers in the little pond and stirs some algae. He acts as if the sensation is not unpleasant, which, in truth, it is. The slime is seething into his fingertips. He finds that he is suddenly craving lobster but ignores the impulse. Jones cannot help but chime in. Really, Cecil? I find that idea terribly unpleasant and terrifying, not reassuring. You always want to keep people guessing. About everything. Nobody is speaking it out loud, but they are wondering what, if anything, they will pass down to the generations beyond them, and what they are contributing right now to the air at this moment, and to the soil, and to the grass, and to the Blue Ox in the hills. Are they adding their pathologies to the inheritance of the world? And are they strong ones or easily curable ones at that? To be weak is to be easily cured, says Lord Burlington, laughing. Strength is a lasting impression, the freedom to roam your own tides of sorrow with no end in sight. The ultimate lasting impression is in an incurable illness. C'mon now, Burlington, says Jones. We know we are all sick today, and I can't get comfortable in these old chairs of yours, and you really must give up your religious concept of revolution. But we will all feel better tomorrow.

THE NOSE SOUGHT OUT TO STUDY ITS PARENT SCIENTIFICALLY.

Your perfectly folded napkins will get you everywhere with me, says Lord Burlington to a pearl-toothed dragon who has recently come to live on his estate. And everywhere it is Swabia. It is Swabia! It is Swabia Day!! Swarms of people have come to Swabia for Swabia Day. All up and down the coast! And, by contrast, in most other places it is merely today when it could just as easily be tomorrow. But Lord Burlington has called up the army. The Swabian army is a good buy these days. There are many Swabian soldiers, women and men, who have chosen careers in the military. The Swabian coast is teeming with visitors. You are in danger; you are always in danger. And it has taken Lord Burlington millions and millions of years to learn to drive a car. The difficulty inherent in managing so many visitors at one time has required us to take the drastic step of calling in the army to keep order. And I miss you, and I want Samantha to be my darling, and I thought everything was going to get better as soon as I put a radish behind her ear. But there is trouble. You are not purple at all, Spider. Lord Burlington is confused. As a precaution, he takes his walking stick out of the trunk of his car. There is a dagger hidden inside the walking stick. And there is something confusing here, after all. The pool of blood is a hurdle. The pool of blood is a longstanding hurdle that will have to be overcome if Lord Burlington is to learn to drive a car. If Lord Burlington is to learn to drive a car, then the collar will come down. But you wouldn't put a collar on that dear Dragon, would you? asks Samantha. Nonetheless, Lord Burlington is old enough and wise enough to know that revealing his plans too early will get him nowhere in the end. He grasps the latest draft of the newly translated *Bible of The Species* a little more tightly. It is Swabia Day today, Samantha, and I don't like it one bit, says Lord Burlington. I love your new car, Burlington. What did you pay for it? interrupts Tom Terrific. Either a lot more or a lot less than I will tell you I paid, laughs Burlington. There is a lot of smoke on the Swabian highways these days. The smoke comes almost exclusively from a single car. You used to love to drive. I never knew how to drive a car. I was honored when I finally got my driver's license. I am afraid you are not as focused as you need to be to drive a car, sir. Sir, I am afraid we will have to terminate our lesson for the day. Lord Burlington's driving instructor puts his foot on the emergency brake and stops the car. And there is a question that needs to be answered about what exactly is going on in Swabia that day. You were hoping to hear that the potion is good? That potions are workable stuff, perhaps? That there is terrible trouble underfoot? That all designs are bad? That there is a beady-eyed peacock on the loose? In fact, there is a beady-eyed peacock on the loose because there has been a mass escape from the Swabian National Petting Zoo. There is danger afoot; there is always danger afoot. You are my one true love, Burlington, says Samantha. She has taken off her silver slippers and has floated very slowly over the top of the gazebo. This car is beautiful, Tom Terrific thinks, as he puts his foot on the gas and steers the car down the wide open Swabian highway...

THE PARASITIC INVADER SOUGHT OUT TO STUDY
THE PRINCIPLES OF WHICH ALL BODIES EXIST
SCIENTIFICALLY.

But to accomplish this, the parasitic invader needed to overcome a hurdle. And not just one but many, and many long-standing ones at that. The blood was a long-standing hurdle, for example, as was virtue, as was a good buy, as was a good driving instructor, as was a pearl-toothed dragon, as was life on earth in general. I must admit that because of the parasitic invader, because of its very existence, because of its very capability of existing, that I know—truly—I am always in danger. There are many cars now coming down the mountain, and there is smoke on the Swabian highway, and Mr. Jones, like myself, has found himself to be an excellent driver, although truly there is no one like him. He loves the feeling of the wind while racing. The slick, planar feeling of moving while in a car. The human crime of smoke and exhaust. And a car is a good buy these days. And there are swarms of people out on the road for Swabia Day. Today is today is today. Today is Swabia Day!! Today I have replaced my black flag with a blue one, and it's whipping and slicing the wind, and it is cold and graceful, and it looks just perfect over my roof. And my roof looks out over the ocean. Today I love my job. I love my job as Pulp and Sight Supervisor at the Swabian Paper Mill, I love the sight, sound, touch, taste, and smell of paper. And I love working for a company that is devoted to virtue: endless, endless growth. But unfortunately for me, and for the other citizens of Swabia, including the men and women in the military, the roads are crowded today and stifling. This is because there has been a sort of accident. It's hard to say because it's hard to know the dispensation of activities or lack of dispensations that have caused this accident to occur. It would seem that everything has escaped from the petting zoo. When the zoo first came into being it was well-designed by a famous team of architects and sanctioned heartily by the acting mayor and it had excellent blueprints (or seeds of thought) and was given great size and visible strength, great form and order, and then the animals arrived, as did the monsters, and the zoo's development was considered healthy and complete. But now because of this public emergency, it would appear that such is not the case. However, the Swabian standing army and reserves are on it. Thanks to our ingenuity and our stratagems we are able to cope well here with life as we know it to be, as well as plan for any possible contingencies that could ever arise during the course of life itself. But when Jones sees the tasers, which look so much like the lights of the planets, of the cosmos, of the orbiting stars themselves, he feels a heave of sympathy. The dragon is cornered alongside a bare dirt patch off the shoulder of the road. He or she is growling and he or she is losing her teeth and he or she is losing her strength and his or her will to cope and his or her will to be a very part of this world at all. He or she could, after all, will himself or herself into being extinct. He or she could decide to no longer be a part of the system. And I see Mr. Jones and the driving instructor pull to the side of the road. I see Jones give a good, starched tug to his striped suit and I see the driving instructor lighting a fig cigarette. The driving instructor is wearing a soupy looking sweater. I see the dragon blink his or her eyelashes in confusion or fear or pain from the smoke that has gotten too close. Today the air is suddenly so noxious. Mr. Jones and the driving instructor are negotiating with a few officers for the dragon's very life. They appear to be winning. And the dragon's 10-foot collar, made of ubiquitous surveillance technology, is being removed by two army men.

This is sympathy in action. The desire to save what is already alive. To keep it alive. To let it be as it was meant to be simply by virtue of being born. That is care in action. Today, right in front of me, right in front of my eyes, our self-serving nature is turning into an endowing compassionate nature, and thus every attribute of every living being is being given the possibility of the virtue of growth. It is happening because of a collapse in the zoo. This is how and when it happens. Does this mark a beginning, an end, or a continuation of something? We have chased off the parasitic invader, right? In my manifesto I note: *The parasitic invader is smart, adroit, and adept. It gives a huff, a noxious bluster, a white writhing glottal heave, a nest of splintering excretions. It hefts its muscular biceps, checks its cancerous helix, its muggy temper, twists its heart like a timer. It is a master of co-opting. Its first task will be to don the mask of care.*

THE MONSTER sought out to study ITS BIRTH SCIENTIFICALLY.

Back behind the pool on Lord Burlington's estate, there is a very large pool-house. The poohouse is actually very modern, architecturally speaking. Yet life around the poolhouse is an entirely different story. In fact, the whole story is what it is when it is told. But you have to begin at the beginning to understand, and at the beginning there are seeds, and at the beginning there were more seeds than anyone could count. And you know that, Burlington, I know you do. No, there is only weakness, Tom Terrific laughs. There is only weakness when the wicked are suspended in violent ways. But I bought you a beautiful orchid at the store just the other day. Yet nobody agrees with me that the orchid is beautiful. The orchid is a shade of blue that has never been seen in Swabia before. An import. An imported goose orchid, to be specific. And because it is a special day and because the next war, or the coming war, has not yet begun and because there are more and more imported goose orchids showing up at Swabian outlet malls. You will come to my pool party at nine o'clock tonight, says Lord Burlington to Tom Terrific. You will bring plenty of imported goose orchids and clam blossoms and plenty of ordinary things too: a bucket, a broom, a sock, a noose, a new religion, a lantern, a pillow, well, okay, maybe not a pillow, but I don't believe in myself anymore. Hey, you have to believe in yourself when the spirit is present, when the spirit is afoot, man, chimes in Cecil from a corner of the poolhouse. He inhales deeply from the fig cigarette he is smoking and starts to laugh. It seems that Cecil is attempting to commit himself to new things these days, to new ways of being, as it were, and the change has brought him a certain measure of self-satisfaction. But then, as the fig cigarette smoke reaches his bloodstream, he starts to feel less well, or rather, less sure about his position, his future. He is lying on his back in a corner of the very large and very modern poolhouse on Lord Burlington's estate. And what has become of my life! Then Cecil puts his face in his hands and starts to cry because he is actually really sad and the world is actually really, really hard. I am all grown up, cries Cecil. You really must come to the pool party, too, Cecil, says Lord Burlington. I have grown up. I have grown up, yells Cecil, over and over again. I wish that boy would shut up. I am trying to sleep. For heaven's sake, it's perfectly fine to be grown up. And even if it weren't, there's no need to cry about it. I just wanted what I wanted when I wanted it, says Mr. Jones to Esmeralda, who is, at this moment, his one and only true and dutiful daughter. Things seem to have gotten a bit out of control at Burlington's? Eh, Esmeralda? Mr. Jones closes his eyes, and begins silently repeating the affirmations he says to himself every night before he goes to sleep. *I used to spend my time on a piece of land...A grassy meadow...I lived on a hill and there was a great Blue Ox on a grassy meadow...I used to put my feet up and do all kinds of work in my mind...In the back of my mind, but I was already dead...It was all kinds of work...It was the kind of work that induced pain and suffering...You can go on in just this way, if you want to...You can go on and feel humble and feel fleet and feel the ways of the world and feel the ways of the world crumble... You can go on and on and you can pretend you like it...* But you do like it this way, Mr. Jones. You always have. And that is why you are the way you are...dead. Pardon me. *Doctor Rat at your service. I was crumbling...I was feeling a little, how shall I say it, let down...I needed things to be good, but I was a bad man...I once made a bad meal for the tarantula who lived in my house...Do you remember our tarantula, Esmeralda...The one who lived far away, but near enough to come and go as it pleased...And I wish I was wise, too...I really wish I'd never been born...* Meanwhile, back at the poolhouse, Cecil has come up with a plan to feel less grown-up. I will climb to the top of that tree over there, thinks Cecil. The one that is so tall and green. The one that grows right behind Lord Burlington's pool. I will climb to the highest branch of that tree and dive in the pool, and I will do this for my own good health and happiness.

THE DISCOVERED SOUGHT OUT TO STUDY THEIR EXPOSURE SCIENTIFICALLY.

You've been waiting too long for this day, I'm afraid, Honorable, says Lord Burlington. Therefore, your level of anticipation is too high. Therefore, you will never be happy. You hang your head. You talk about the war as if it were a thing to be considered, to be conceived of. You talk about the war as if it were, well, something other than what it is. And there is a hat suspended in the air. And there is a running around the room backwards. A sheep and a dog and a camel and an angel with wings. But you will get away from here in the end, Lord Burlington says. In the end, you will get away from this place and forget all about me, and there will be no tomorrow and no one, but no one, will remember that I have ever lived. And it was like that, once upon a time. In the high hills above the Swabian coast. The erosion of the Swabian cliffs by the sea was a concern. And you can hear a necklace falling from a cliff. I swear, says Tom Terrific, it is quiet enough in here tonight to hear a necklace falling from a cliff. The green, green sea. The Swabian coast at night. There is a real fear, though, says Dr. Honorable, shuddering, of, how shall I put it, exposure, when the Swabian cliffs are reduced to dust. There is something different in the air in Swabia tonight. Come, Terrific, have a seat beside me in the gazebo. Sit back, relax, and take in the view of the landed dog statue. The imitation coat of arms. The fish pond. And all I was trying to say was that I love you. Hardly, huffs Lord Burlington. Religion belongs to the masses. Religion, religious beliefs, religious personas and disguises belong to all of Swabia, to each and every ordinary Swabian citizen, and that's why I say this so... Ahem!... forcefully. But you used to be an excellent swimmer, Terrific. You used to cut up hammers and swell nails and make pastry, all right out of the back of your room. And, at this point, do even remember what you are? What you could have been? You could have been great, you know, and there is no tomorrow and there is nothing left in this room for me to share. But, and this is not so easily put, says Dr. Honorable, I love you. I was simply trying to say, I love you. I love you, says Mr. Jones from high on a hill, from a place both deep within and utterly without the earth. And it is not a coincidence that this night describes the folding and the luxury and the necessary accommodations that put a war to bed, that put your war to bed, that put your hatred and mis-timing and mimicry and gossip in the ground. I love you. And this is very easy to say, as easy as holding a bicycle in one hand and a fully mature horsetomato plant in the other. And I love you, and I say good afternoon in the most delicate way imaginable. But you are a jerk, Burlington. And most people can see that plain and clear, if they care to look, if they are courageous enough to look. If they care about seeing him at all, you mean, says Dr. Honorable, gently. Come over here for a minute, Terrific, come into the gazebo where the light is better, I'd like to take a look at your throat. The level of discomfort, of shame, you've been experiencing is astonishing and overwhelming and not more than a little bit staggering. It's too much for anyone to bear, Terrific. Come over here. There is a good, well-lit spot in the gazebo. It is summer in Swabia. There is a green garden growing under a bank of trees. For the first time that anyone can remember, every animal in the petting zoo is free. There is no coercion and no sticking up for what's wrong and no sitting and then standing and then propping and then falling to rash and harsh exchanges. The fish pond is a thing of beauty and a wonder to behold. And hold your hands up, says, Dr. Honorable, just like this, and then breathe. And then, one day, one day, it's as if...as if... and there is nothing, but somehow peace reigns supreme. And that's the cure, whispers Dr. Honorable, and it really is as easy as that.

THE REMOTE AND BOOKISH PHYSICIAN SOUGHT OUT TO STUDY MEDICINE SCIENTIFICALLY.

Tom Terrific, the Acting Mayor of All Swabia, was feeling ill again and thought he had gotten sick under the big tent at the circus, or at a naval ceremony, or was it the legally imported pollens at the Swabian Botanical Gardens? His stomach felt queasy. It was all very unnamable, very nauseating, very disquieting. His tongue was hurting too much. The sky seemed parceled and disconnected. The clouds were jagged. All teeth. He found it hard to swallow. He found it hard to smile. He found it hard to breathe. He found it hard to walk. This was hurting the city's infrastructure and overall morale, which is never good for business at the outlet malls or outdoor market. People come from all over for that market. And there was the overall matter of debt to consider. His illness was hard to diagnose. It could have been the clam blossoms, it could have been the imported fig cigars, it could have been the rotten walking stick, it could have been general malaise, it could have been the bad air, the bad water, the fire on the hills, the fire in the house, it could have been man's hatred of man, man's hatred of woman, woman's hatred of man, man's hatred of nature, it could have been that slightly expired gooseberry wine, it could have been that cloying conscience, it could have been that stab in the back, it could have been that can of horsetomato sauce, it could have been the viral petting zoo, it could have been genetics, it could have been genetic manipulation, it could have been an accident, it could have been a bad batch of fruit orchids, it could have been yesterday, or the day before that, or the years before that. Had something been growing all this time? Tell me the whole story, says the physician to Tom Terrific, gesturing to a nice wide chair. The bookish physician is new to Swabia and has a less orthodox practice. He first likes to meet with his patients on a calm, temperate day, always outdoors, always somewhere where the grass is lively and there is a good view over the green hills and cliffs. The physician likes to take daily walks. He likes to walk on the soil. It's all about the soil. Everything is about the soil. He likes walking in his sandals over the fresh young shoots of the gooseberry bushes and orchids. From where they are sitting, the mayor and the physician have a wonderful view of the Blue Ox as she is standing out in a meadow with a long purple stem of barleygrass hanging from her mouth. It's all very musical. And the musical notes are falling. The physician repeats himself, as he often does: tell me the whole story, he says to his patient, the mayor. How can I tell you the whole story? says Tom Terrific, taking off his shoes and socks in order to feel the nice warm air on his feet. I am only one man. And I have only been alive for a little while yet, not like Lord Burlington. Did you know it took him a million years just to learn how to shift into first gear? What can I tell you? It could have been the clam blossoms, or the stale fig cigars, or too much walking, or a bad walking stick, or the many parallels between the ill-health of my body and the ill-health of the entire world and the entire civic body as a whole. How can I say? And how can I say now, especially as I don't believe in myself anymore? The physician nods with emotion, but still takes notes on a clipboard. Well, Mayor, the world is really, really hard these days. And there's a lot of information floating around. Of course, the soil is bad now too. It's all about the soil. *Dr. Honorable at your service.* The bookish physician recoils instantly, looks momentarily like an ant, and begins to sneer like a spoiled boy. I told you, already, Honorable, to stay off my turf, man, seriously, Pal-O-Mine. This is not your domain anymore. Now there are two physicians in town and one of us is going to be better than the other. Dr. Honorable is horrified. You reproach me because my medicine is not like yours? You cry out against me, and in all your fragility? You cry out against me—but that is the fault of your understanding, not mine! The bookish physician claims that he only wants to cure his patient. The acting mayor is rolling on the ground now, wearing a nice suit. His teeth are clamping down on his tongue. He rolls as if he were putting out a fire. He rolls as if he is struggling against himself. He is clutching his stomach. It feels yellow, green, red, purple, it feels bilious, putrid, lightheaded, it feels committed to its own discomfort. Meanwhile, the two doctors continue to have their dispute. That's amusing coming from you, Honorable. You pretend that your work is well-rooted in experiment and evidence. But I know when the right time comes, the young shoots of your clever ideas, your clever advice, your clever medicines, your clever cures, will have their time, just as mine will. It's all about the soil. New beginnings. *The new ways of seeing the new.* You're a real dim wicket, Honorable. Dr. Honorable is unflustered. He snaps a purple orchid out of the ground and smells it, then tosses it out over a cliff and watches it arc down toward the ocean. The fires are back on the hills. He should be doing something about this. The Acting mayor of All Swabia wishes to be cured. Tom Terrific wishes to commit himself to a new way of being. Or at least to consider a commitment. He rolls around on the ground and clutches pieces of the meadows in his fists. He's all heaving and dirt. It could have been the circus or it could have been the zoo. The exotic, out-of-town animals. That big green dragon that needed to be constantly fed. It could have been the dyes in his new coat. He wants to be cured, but he is not pleased that his diagnosis would require him to be discovered and exposed. He is not pleased to have to grow up. Your own personal wounds do not upset me, says Doctor Honorable to the bookish physician. Tom Terrific, observing the dispute, wonders if he should step in and mediate. If he could just feel a little better, think a little more clearly, have a little more information to go on, then he could decide who is right and who isn't. There's no sticking up for a wrong idea. But he is struck by an awful thought that he is hesitant to admit. As he watches the two doctors argue, kick the ground, he thinks to himself (although still clutching his gut), Perhaps you like it this way. Perhaps you like things to stay the same. Perhaps you always have.

AUTHORITY SOUGHT OUT TO STUDY ITS BASIS SCIENTIFICALLY.

The whole problem with growing horsetomatoes in the spring is that there are no garlic plants, and folding occurs early, and when there is light, the length of the shadow also grows, but, hang it, you are not listening to me, growls, Tom Terrific. No one is listening to me and I don't know why. Am I being too precious? Tom Terrific is the Acting Mayor of All Swabia, and he cannot believe his ears. The way the wind blows. The noise. *You are flat on your feet. You can run but you can't hide. You hear what they tell you. Or what? You'd better believe it, man. You hear and if you had your hands out and you hear... and you hear.* Tom Terrific is standing on a grassy meadow. The rolling Swabian hills are beautiful in the afternoon light. They are, in fact, a sight to behold. There is even a giant Blue Ox in the distance, and an abundance of wild barleygrass. Tom Terrific is sitting on a blanket on a grassy meadow, and he is more than a little bit angry. It has been a long while since he has had time to be alone, and now his opportunity is being spoiled because of the noise. A terrible conflict has occurred. A conflict, an argument, a competition, has occurred, at some point, on the grassy meadow where Tom Terrific sits, and there are echoes of it still resounding in the air. *I am at home when I hear you call. And, yes, sir, you are always right. Curse that day. The summer is here and then you leave me and I have nowhere to go. I am on my own and I am too scared to even put my hat in the air. You blame me for everything. You are acting just like a prince or princess. I have nowhere to go.* Tom Terrific is bummed out. He has made an amazing picnic lunch, and now it's too noisy for him to eat. *We were fighting for our very survival. The skills on display with this knife, this stiletto, in my hand will astonish, frighten, and, ultimately, entice you. And the way I argue. But I can win. I know I can win. I have my heart to protect after all. I have my reputation to consider. I have my heart and my eyes and my ears but my blood is landing, pooling, all over the place and this is all wrong, but I am right, and this is all wrong and I am right, and this is all wrong, and I am right. And I have the cure here, and I have the cure over here.* Tom Terrific has brought watercress and gooseberry fruitcake and horsetomato quiche and vegetable sushi for lunch, and now he fears that all hope for a pleasant meal is lost. *And I am on the corner and it is hot. And I hope you get home at a decent hour. And I hope there is glory and holding on. You are a pin, or a pill. You take it from me.* Oh well, thinks Tom, I might as well give up and go home. And now, you see what I mean, says Mr. Jones, flatly. I think he gets it, says Esmeralda, Mr. Jones's daughter. And because he gets it, it wouldn't surprise me one bit if everyone else starts to get it too.

THE PATENTLY FALSE SOUGHT OUT TO STUDY GREAT PERIODS OF PROMISE SCIENTIFICALLY.

This was, of course, a paradox. As if you could hold your own heart on a string. Or look down your own throat. See tomorrow coming. But it is that easy. The Mysterious Udolpho was making a nice sum of money teaching watercolor classes. He continued his attempts to instruct and reform the patently false ideas of his students. He read them an old love letter.

> *Just put your wars, all of them, to bed. And when I say all of them, I mean the ones you have against yourself, and the ones you wage outwardly, and the ones you wage on the land, and against the land, and all others. The Swabian coastline is eroding. The Swabian mollusk is endangered. And yet the ocean, from a distance, still looks so nice. The sun is up today. There are necklaces at the bottom of the sea. There are old rolodexes and initiation rites at the bottom of the sea. There are seeds and there are bones and there is blood. And what a pretty ocean. There are sapphires at the bottom of the sea. And when the moon is reflected on the Swabian coast, all the sharks, whales, scallops and scarabs start to do important things.*

Esmeralda has returned from her trip to the snowy alps, where she had intended to ski and relax but instead had found herself becoming inspired to paint. She sees her art primarily as a record-keeping device. She wishes to record everything that's disappearing, or is in the process of disappearing, before it is gone. Therefore, when she paints, she must reflect on herself and the world, and their causal relationship, very heavily. This brings her a staggering amount of shame. She puts on her smock and stands at the very peak of the Swabian cliffs and paints pictures of antlers, drying heaps of uncultivated turnips, the endangered Swabian mollusk, the weakening branches, the conflicts that the people have put in the ground, the blue fire on the hills, the real fear, and the eroding coastline. And what about the staggering amount of shame? Mr. Jones is wearing an apron and making pastry for his daughter. His hands are covered with cornflower. His fingertips and his pockets are studded with specks of dough. He gives Esmeralda wise, fatherly advice. Do you remember, little one, when you were such a tiny hurricane? Do you remember the summer we spent sitting in the gazebo at Lord Burlington's estate, do you remember seeing fall approaching in the backyard, do you remember sitting next to the fish pond, and all you could do was stir the air? Change the atmosphere for the better? Emit ripples and alter the currents of the whole entire world we live in? As we know, everything is interconnected. It's that easy. It's that simple. And that's the simple cure. Do you remember what you are? Esmeralda sips her father's hand-squeezed limeade and wrings a soggy piece of mint between her fingers. I know, father. But if it's any reassurance to you at all, I'm getting back on track. I've studied myself quite closely. I have even taken up watercoloring. Mr. Jones makes his daughter a feast. Orchid roulade, stews of figs and edible weeds, marzipan. Esmeralda and Mr. Jones make a wonderful family of two, for they have much in common. Father, I'm thinking of starting a manifesto on how to paint. There are people in my watercolor class who act like they want to learn, but their art is terrible, really. They can only paint ash and strange, blocky images of dictators and the stubble of this and the stubble of that and this sort of gristle and that sort of muddy temperament and concrete examples of coarse egoism, and war, and competition, and corruption, and the wrong side winning (or actually stealing), and it's all really really awful. Their art aims for escape value and wide appeal. Their color palettes are truly bilious. Or sometimes they're too fluorescent or just saccharine. And these images seem too easy to make, or too hard. They lug these gleaming, monument-sized canvases to class and then just add stains to their artistic vision. It's is truly reactionary, ignorant stuff. It needs to be exposed. There needs to be an outcry! Esme, says Jones, I'm not saying that these people aren't dangerous, but don't let them hold you back. When Esmeralda returns to class, she dabs at her canvas with her own breath. She paints the air picking up, a gentle drizzle. And that's the cure. It's that simple.

THE TRUTH SOUGHT OUT TO STUDY DECEPTIVE PHYSICIANS SCIENTIFICALLY.

Fly me to the moon, Terrific, said Samantha one day quite out of the blue. It was the beginning of summer, the beginning of spring, the beginning of new things, the way the beginning of new things was always the beginning of, well, new things. Thus, replied Tom Terrific, you don't have to get angry. What's wrong with you today, Tom? I was merely trying to inform you that you have gooseberry all over your mouth and hands and you really need to drink more liquids and get more tree shade and there is not a place in the city or town for the likes of you when you act that way or when you look at me that way. And your enemies are far from here. The war is over. You have nothing to worry about, Tom, I swear. I swear, Samantha, I used to know you better. I used to know better than to know you better than I do. But I belong to an ancient cult, says Tom. An ancient political cult and this is all getting to be a little too, dare I say, ritualistic for me. I should have woken up crying and instead I find myself in the most peculiar situation I have ever found myself in before. It's a real pickle. What am I going to do, Samantha? I am so many things, just the way you always tell me, and I can only feel your pity and I can only think of my days in the Swabian navy fondly and never in any other way. What's wrong with me? What's going on with me? Here, hand me my brush, Samantha. And, Lord Burlington, says Tom, the way you used to lie all the time, and now you only tell the truth, but you file lawsuits all the time. You use courts of law for your own gain. Only to protect myself, or to protect you, says Lord Burlington. I have valuable things on my estate that are constantly under attack by heathens, by the people who claim to have owned them first. That is, by the masses.

You know that, Terrific. Samantha, darling, for example, these horseto-mato plants and gooseberry bushes and wild barleygrass are beautiful to the eye, aren't they? Why, just think, if they got out in the world somehow, then anyone could plant and grow them. They'd be boring and worthless then. Right? Was I talking to you? I was talking to you. I wasn't talking to you. I was trying to talk to Tom. I only love Tom. I am ridiculous, I know, but I have decided I only love Tom, and I want to talk to him all the time. Tom are you listening to me? Lord Burlington, says Terrific, it's like you always used to say. The way you used to tell us. Remember when I first started working for you, Burlington? Lord Burlington, you are a peach. You know that don't you? You are a fig. A nut. A real plum. And the view from your estate could not be better. They used to call this the heath, my boy, grumbles Burlington. And maybe they will again. Who knows? But, now, you are walking backwards and there is a purple spider behind your back, shadowing you, at all times and your way actually is the highway and soon you will be completely out of earshot of Samantha and everyone else who has ever cared about you. Congratulations! Though that sentiment may be a touch premature. But, have no fear, you just continue on, my boy. You just continue on and on and everything is going to be fine. I know it's all going to work out in the end. Why, when I close my eyes I can see your name on any number of valuable patents right now. Where do you want to go for dinner? *Dr. Honorable at your service.* Someone called me some time ago, I'm afraid. And I am truly sorry that it has taken me as long as it has to get here. I'm not too late, am I? I mean... Then, suddenly, there is a fire. And everyone runs. There is an explosion, suddenly, and smoke, and flames. Lord Burlington's gazebo has spontaneously combusted, and everything is starting all over again, that is, everything has, at this point, the potential to start all over again. Right from the beginning, the flames could be seen... There was a gazebo on fire... Many things, including a gazebo, on Lord Burlington's estate were on fire... And the flames can be seen for miles. Today there is a big beautiful Blue Ox on a hill. Yesterday there was a big beautiful Blue Ox on a hill. And tomorrow there will be a big beautiful Blue Ox on a hill. You just have to sort of feel your way out of it, says Dr. Honorable. That is really the only way to do it, even though it seems hard. And it is hard. Why, in fact, it's a revolution! Anyhow, one has to recognize that these things *do* happen. And, indeed, the unexpected *does* occur... I'm sorry you are feeling badly about everything. But hang in there and take two of these gooseberry tablets millions and millions of times daily, or as often as you'd like. And never, ever hesitate to call me if you find yourself in trouble again.

FEELING BETTER SOUGHT OUT TO STUDY FEELING WORSE SCIENTIFICALLY.

Now there were too many deceptive physicians crawling about Swabia. They were touting all sorts of cures. Balneology this and balneology that. Balneology with lemons and sprigs of grass. Or balneology and eating sand. Eating salad. Eating sugar. A bath of garlic. A shoehorn made of lab-manufactured agate for one's terrible confused life, one's terrible accursed and vulnerable existence. Balneology and a sprig of rose, a dose of a shotglass of a needle of a stamp of…and too much sand in one's lungs was a good thing, and eating a peanut butter sandwich along with your balneology. *But do avoid…* And they acted as if such schemes were not such a terrible curse on the beautiful water. The land was in disarray, the rolling grass was ragged and no longer a sight to behold. The Blue Ox was getting too skinny and she was lying on the dirt floor of a cave with her sons beside her. Tom Terrific, the Acting Mayor of All Swabia, felt really terrible about it all. Felt ashamed really. He had focused too much on Swabia's flourishing centers of commerce, on Swabian isolationism, on bottling its waters, its great healing mineral springs, the healing powers of Swabia. And so a lot of tourists came. And this of course resulted in… and this had attracted one too many doctors looking to make a quick dime. The tourists came like ducklings. They came with their miserably earned money. They came with their cash elitism. And so the country was sick. It was really sick. It was shredded, and there were yellow fires burning on the hills. Tom Terrific gets it. He finally got it. He finally gets it. But this is only making him feel worse rather than better. Or is it the opposite? Is there a slight bit of pleasure that comes with a diagnosis, even if it's a disappointing one? And where are the doctors? I mean, the ones who don't just service the princes or the lords or the acting mayors, but the towns and the countries and the land? And more importantly, where is the doctor who can treat the Blue Ox? For she is most important. Tom Terrific returns to his old gooseberry tree, which is holding steady, neither dying nor growing. Despite the land being in disarray. He returns to the tree to think, just like when he was younger. It is a little ragged now and drops its berries onto the barleygrass with a nearly inaudible sound. Tom Terrific remembers the days when he didn't have much to do. He would walk without hurrying to this spot. He would stuff his pockets with dog orchids and spider orchids, and then empty them. He would eat apples under the tree. He would spend hours honing the perfect walking stick and then leave it behind to lie on the ground. Once he even hung a rose-colored necklace on a tree branch. He was good at such gestures of romantic attention and humility. But now the land seems to hold nothing but the remnants of struggle and conflict, too many of them, personal conflicts, and interpersonal ones, and great ones and naval ones and professional and international ones and armed ones. Or this is right and I am wrong, he thinks. Or this is wrong and I am right. And he can't grin. And if he can't grin, then the city will really sink. The Blue Ox is preparing a stew of nettles for her sons. And there are a few spring onions left. She knows so much about these hills that she might as well be a written record, a hidden scroll, a holy book, a barometer. But too many people treat her like a keepsake. Or a beautiful view. She lingers on the barleygrass and thinks to herself, if only more people would listen to me. But no one listens to me and I don't know why. However, despite being thin she holds no shame. She still wears a gold necklace around her neck. It is classy and wound like ivy. She still wears amethysts around her ankles and threads jewelry out of the mother-of-pearl she picks up on the coast. She makes lanterns out of seaweed and hangs them on the roof of her cave. She still gives her sons nothing but the best kind of love. Tom Terrific is feeling badly about himself again. He is doubting himself. His head is full of all sorts of pressures because he is trying to think about all things in existence at once and then decide upon a course of action. But the Blue Ox is mending herself, she truly is. And she will not abide this state of disarray forever. She will change things. And if anyone can do it, it is the Blue Ox. And this is good for all of us. It truly is. I believe in the Blue Ox. She will make us believe in ourselves.

THE ISLANDS IN THE SEA SOUGHT OUT TO STUDY SWABIA SCIENTIFICALLY.

The violence of Swabia. The threat on the coast. The coat of arms is an imitation. I used to know an architect, a balneologist, a cider maker. I used to know all of these professional types of people because the world was purple and life was very rich and full and exciting. And how do you get your horsetomatoes to grow so well? asks Mr. Jones. He is muttering to himself from underneath a patch of grass high on a rolling Swabian hill. And everyone thinks they've forgotten about me. And, well, they haven't. They just haven't. They just think they have. It's as simple as that. But the parting of the ways… the parting of the worlds…

THE WRONG SIDE SOUGHT OUT TO STUDY JUSTICE SCIENTIFICALLY.

Izetta is in the alley again, wearing next to nothing, trying on her crown. She is in a cream-colored slip. She has been doing nothing all day but shucking gooseberries into a wooden bowl and dicing heirloom tomatoes. And the evenings have consisted of nothing but a flood of dinner guests and almost all of them important men, most of them men, architects, physicians, mayors, police chiefs, and lounge-abouts, and the occasional buffoon or quiche-lover or raisin-eater or artist or prince, and of course Mr. Jones himself, and she the only woman in the house and often the only woman at the table. And do you remember that one guy? The one who called himself Lord Burlington, who hogged all the horsesauce and rice, and who preferred to eat all his food on a silver dish, who sprinkled watercress into just about everything? Damn, his coat was loud. Izetta feels lonely today. And today is today. And today could be lost or won. And you just continue going on and everything is going to be okay in the end. You just continue and it's all going to work out. In the end. You have to just keep sweeping the alleyway and clearing space and singing to the cats. You have to believe in the great upheaval no matter what. You can't be afraid to say it, to think it. Despite all the guests coming and going from the house, coming for dinner, leaving behind their napkins, leaving the dishes encrusted, the silverware handled, the leftover wine, leaving their good and bad seeds of thought, their reliance on the past, their reliance on the future, their hope for the present, their recommendations for vitamins, the ashes of their fig cigarettes in an amber ashtray, and don't forget the damage that the smoke does to the lampshade in the den, the damage done to the deck of cards, leaving behind their conversation and their compliments and their pro-posed remedies or their dour outlooks, their facts, their knowledge about this or of that, their desires to be on the winning side. And Izetta's heart is soaked again. You just have to ride out the moss and toxins in the water and pollutants in the alley. But Izetta has a particular strength. Despite all of this, and many of these guests have brought Izetta roses these past few weeks and other kinds of flowers, no one has ever said anything to her about the crown sitting on the top of her head. No one has done anything to indicate that they've even seen it. And Izetta is fed up. She feels particu-late and stealthy. She wants to throw today's uncooked stew in the gutter of the alley. Hurl her spoon at the dumpster. Yell at all the tar on the ground. She wants to throw her own crown in the ring. Really, she wants to leave the alley. She wants to go off on a trip with the purple spider, an adventure, just the two of them. And experience all the elements and all the pillars of virtue the world has to offer. And on the way they could collect a following of sorts, but not a true following, and definitely not an army, in the sense that no one should really follow anyone else. But nevertheless, they could build a lot of momentum. Like a hurricane. And it could be gentle too. A drizzle, or a vine slowly growing down the side of a building. You just have to take a good, deep breath in. And together Izetta and the purple spider would have no fear. No unnecessary fear. And as Izetta pictures this in her head she imagines herself untangling the knots in her hair, she pictures garlands growing everywhere about the alley. And they don't look like any-thing you've ever seen. The elements are returning, and wild barleygrass and the right kind of buildings. And she and the purple spider will travel to Dalmatia and Salmatia, to the Swabian coast—anywhere they wish to go, really. And on her travels she will try all sorts of new things: gooseberry gravy, gooseberry wine, gooseberry bread, gooseberry pie. They will collect listeners. And when people protest their bald language, their confidence, their elaborate style of dress, and their certainty, they will reply back (but all the while avoiding a war of words): There are barometers of disarray all about us and so many, many cures. There are fires in the hills, and even in the most distant corners of your homes; there are places now on this earth where even the dogs will not piss. And the dogs are always a good barometer. You should listen to the dogs. But do not follow us. Do not follow anyone. And even though Izetta's sentiments might be a bit premature, there will still be a new world no matter what. The world will just roll over on its stomach one day and it will be beautiful. The way is no longer blocked. You have nothing to worry about. You cannot be afraid to say it. And you have nothing to worry about. You just have to understand me. I just have to understand what I mean. You just have to trust me. You have nothing to worry about, and worrying will get you nowhere.

Sections of *Man's Wars and Wickedness* are from:

Paracelsus. *Essential Readings*. Berkeley: North Atlantic Books, 1999.

Shiva, Vandana. *Biopiracy: The Plunder of Nature and Knowledge*. Boston: South End Press, 1997.